1/24

ORBITAL

Also by Samantha Harvey

Fiction
The Wilderness
All is Song
Dear Thief
The Western Wind

Nonfiction
The Shapeless Unease: A Year of Not Sleeping

ORBITAL

A NOVEL

SAMANTHA
HARVEY

Grove Press
New York

First published in 2023 in the United Kingdom by Jonathan Cape,
an imprint of Penguin Random House UK.

Published simultaneously in Canada
Printed in the United States of America

This book was set in 11.65-pt. Dante by Alpha Design & Composition
of Pittsfield, NH.

First Grove Atlantic hardcover edition: December 2023

Library of Congress Cataloging-in-Publication data
is available for this title.

ISBN 978-0-8021-6154-3
eISBN 978-0-8021-6155-0

Grove Press
an imprint of Grove Atlantic
154 West 14th Street
New York, NY 10011

Distributed by Publishers Group West

groveatlantic.com

23 24 25 26 27   10 9 8 7 6 5 4 3 2

24 Hours of Earth Orbits With Daylight in the Northern Hemisphere

ORBITAL

Orbit minus 1

Rotating about the earth in their spacecraft they are so together, and so alone, that even their thoughts, their internal mythologies, at times convene. Sometimes they dream the same dreams – of fractals and blue spheres and familiar faces engulfed in dark, and of the bright energetic black of space that slams their senses. Raw space is a panther, feral and primal; they dream it stalking through their quarters.

They hang in their sleeping bags. A hand-span away beyond a skin of metal the universe unfolds in simple eternities. Their sleep begins to thin and some distant earthly morning dawns and their laptops flash the first silent messages of a new day; the wide-awake, always-awake station vibrates with fans and filters. In the galley are the remnants of last night's dinner – dirty forks secured to the table by magnets and chopsticks wedged in a pouch on the wall. Four blue balloons are buoyed on the circulating air, some foil bunting says *Happy Birthday*, it was nobody's birthday but it was a celebration and it was all they had. There's a smear of chocolate on a pair of scissors and a small felt moon on a piece of string, tied to the handles of the foldable table.

Outside the earth reels away in a mass of moonglow, peeling backward as they forge towards its edgeless edge; the tufts of cloud across the Pacific brighten the nocturnal ocean to cobalt. Now there's Santiago on South America's approaching coast in a cloud-hazed burn of gold. Unseen through the closed shutters the trade winds blowing across the warm waters of the Western Pacific have worked up a storm, an engine of heat. The winds take the warmth out of the ocean where it gathers as clouds which thicken and curdle and begin to spin in vertical stacks that have formed a typhoon. As the typhoon moves west towards southern Asia, their craft tracks east, eastward and down towards Patagonia where the lurch of a far-off aurora domes the horizon in neon. The Milky Way is a smoking trail of gunpowder shot through a satin sky.

Onboard the craft it's Tuesday morning, four fifteen, the beginning of October. Out there it's Argentina it's the South Atlantic it's Cape Town it's Zimbabwe. Over its right shoulder the planet whispers morning – a slender molten breach of light. They slip through time zones in silence.

*   *   *

They have each at some point been shot into the sky on a kerosene bomb, and then through the atmosphere in a burning capsule with the equivalent weight of two black bears upon them. They have each steeled their ribcages against the force until they felt the bears retreat, one after the other, and the sky become space, and gravity diminish, and their hair stand on end.

Six of them in a great H of metal hanging above the earth. They turn head on heel, four astronauts (American, Japanese, British, Italian) and two cosmonauts (Russian, Russian); two women, four men, one space station made up of seventeen connecting modules, seventeen and a half thousand miles an hour. They are the latest six of many, nothing unusual about this any more, routine astronauts in earth's backyard. Earth's fabulous and improbable backyard. Turning head on heel in the slow drift of their hurtle, head on hip on hand on heel, turning and turning with the days. The days rush. They will each be here for nine months or so, nine months of this weightless drifting, nine months of this swollen head, nine months of this sardine living, nine months of this earthward gaping, then back to the patient planet below.

Some alien civilisation might look on and ask: what are they doing here? Why do they go nowhere but round and round? The earth is the answer to every question. The earth is the face of an exulted lover; they watch it sleep and wake and become lost in its habits. The earth is a mother waiting for her children to return, full of stories and rapture and longing. Their bones a little less dense, their limbs a little thinner. Eyes filled with sights that are difficult to tell.

Orbit 1, ascending

Roman wakes early. He sloughs off his sleeping bag and swims in the dark to the lab window. Where are we, where are we? Where on earth. It's night and there's land. Into view edges a giant city nebula among reddish-rust-nothing; no, two cities, Johannesburg and Pretoria locked together like a binary star. Just beyond the hoop of the atmosphere is the sun, and in the next minute it will clear the horizon and flood the earth, and dawn will come and go in a matter of seconds before daylight is everywhere at once. Central and East Africa suddenly bright and hot.

Today is his four hundredth and thirty-fourth day in space, a tally arrived at over three different missions. He keeps close count. Of this mission it's day eighty-eight. In a single nine-month mission there are in total roughly five hundred and forty hours of morning exercise. Five hundred morning and afternoon meetings with the American, European and Russian crews on the ground. Four thousand three hundred and twenty sunrises, four thousand three hundred and twenty sunsets. Almost one hundred and eight million miles travelled. Thirty-six Tuesdays, for all that, this being one. Five hundred and forty times of having to swallow toothpaste. Thirty-six changes of T-shirt, a hundred and thirty-five changes of underwear (a fresh set of underwear every day is a storage luxury that can't be afforded), fifty-four clean pairs of socks. Auroras, hurricanes, storms – their numbers unknown but their occurrence certain. Nine full cycles, of course, of the moon, their silver companion moving placidly through its phases while the days go awry. But all the same the moon seen several times a day and sometimes in strange distortion.

To his tally kept on a piece of paper in his crew quarters, Roman will add the eighty-eighth line. Not to wish the time away but to try to tether it to something countable. Otherwise – otherwise the centre drifts. Space shreds time to pieces. They were told this in training: keep a tally each day when you wake, tell yourself *this is the morning of a new day*. Be clear with yourself on this matter. This is the morning of a new day.

And so it is, but in this new day they'll circle the earth sixteen times. They'll see sixteen sunrises and sixteen sunsets, sixteen days and sixteen nights. Roman clasps the handrail by the window to steady himself;

the southern hemisphere stars are fleeting away. You're bound to Coordinated Universal Time, ground crews tell them. Be clear with yourself on this matter, always clear. Look often at your watch to anchor your mind, tell yourself when you wake up: this is the morning of a new day.

And so it is. But it's a day of five continents and of autumn and spring, glaciers and deserts, wildernesses and warzones. In their rotations around the earth in accumulations of light and dark in the baffling arithmetic of thrust and attitude and speed and sensors, the whip-crack of morning arrives every ninety minutes. They like these days when the brief bloom of daybreak outside coincides with their own.

In this last minute of darkness the moon is near-full and low to the glow of atmosphere. It's as if night has no idea it's about to be obliterated by day. Roman has a sense of himself a few months hence staring from his bedroom window at home, moving aside his wife's array of dried – and to him unnameable – flowers, forcing open the condensated and stiff casement, leaning into the Moscow air, and seeing it, the same moon, like a souvenir he's brought back from a holiday somewhere exotic. But it's just for a moment and then the sight of this moon from the space station – lying squashed and low beyond the atmosphere, not really above them but across, like an equal – is everything, and that brief comprehension he had of his bedroom, his home, is gone.

There was a lesson at school about the painting *Las Meninas*, when Shaun was fifteen. It was about how the painting disoriented its viewer and left them not knowing what it was they were looking at.

It's a painting inside a painting, his teacher had said – look closely. Look here. Velázquez, the artist, is in the painting, at his easel, painting a painting, and what he's painting is the king and queen, but they're outside of the painting, where we are, looking in, and the only way we know they're there is because we can see their reflection in a mirror directly in front of us. What the king and queen are looking at is what we're looking at – their daughter and her ladies-in-waiting, which is what the painting is called – *Las Meninas*, 'The Ladies-in-Waiting'. So what is the real subject of this painting – the king and queen (who are being painted and whose white reflected faces, though small, are in the centre background), their daughter (who is the star in the middle, so bright and blonde in the gloom), her ladies- (and dwarves and chaperones and dog) in-waiting, the furtive man mid-stride in the doorway in the background who seems to be bringing a message, Velázquez (whose presence as the painter is declared by the fact of him being in the painting, at his easel painting what is a picture of the king and queen but what also might be *Las Meninas* itself), or is it us, the viewers, who occupy the same position as the king and queen, who are looking in, and who are being looked at by both Velázquez and the infant princess and, in reflection, by the king and queen? Or, is the subject art itself (which is a set of illusions and tricks and artifices within life), or life itself (which is a set of illusions and tricks and artifices within a consciousness that is trying to understand life through perceptions and dreams and art)?

Or – the teacher said – is it just a painting about nothing? Just a room with some people in it and a mirror?

To Shaun, who, at fifteen, did not want to take art classes and already knew he wanted to be a fighter pilot, this lesson was the height and depth of all futility. He didn't like the painting particularly and he didn't care what it was of. Probably, yes, it was just a room with some people and a mirror, but he didn't even care enough to put his hand up and say that. He was drawing geometric doodles on his notepad. Then he drew a picture of somebody being hanged. The girl sitting next to him saw those doodles and nudged him and raised her brow and smiled, a small fugitive smile, and when she became his wife many years later she gave him a postcard of *Las Meninas*, it being, to her, an emblem of their first real exchange. And when, years after that, he was away in Russia preparing to go into space, she wrote in a cramped hand on the back of the postcard a précis of everything their teacher had said, which he'd entirely forgotten but which she'd remembered with a lucidity that didn't surprise him, because she was the sharpest and most lucid human he'd met.

He has that postcard in his crew quarters. This morning when he wakes up he finds himself staring at it, at all of the possibilities of subject and perspective that his wife wrote out on its reverse. The king, the queen, the maids, the girl, the mirror, the artist. He stares for longer than he's aware. There's the lingering sense of an unfinished dream, something wild in his thoughts. When he climbs out of his sleeping bag and puts on his running gear and goes to the galley for coffee, he catches sight of the distinctive northerly point of Oman jutting into the Persian Gulf, dust clouds over the navy Arabian Sea, the great Indus Estuary, what he knows to be Karachi – invisible now in daylight, but by night a great, complex, cross-hatched grid that reminds him of the doodles he used to do.

According to the arbitrary metric of time they use up here where time is blasted, it's six in the morning. The others are rising.

They look down and they understand why it's called Mother Earth. They all feel it from time to time. They all make an association between the earth and a mother, and this in turn makes them feel like children. In their clean-shaven androgynous bobbing, their regulation shorts and spoonable food, the juice drunk through straws, the birthday bunting, the early nights, the enforced innocence of dutiful days, they all have moments up here of a sudden obliteration of their astronaut selves and a powerful sense of childhood and smallness. Their towering parent ever-present through the dome of glass.

But now, more so. Since Chie came to the galley on Friday evening where they were making dinner, her face colourless with shock, and said, My mother has died. And Shaun let go of his packet of noodles so that it floated above the table, and Pietro swam the three feet towards her, bowed his head and took both of her hands with a choreography so seamless you'd have thought it was prepared, and Nell muttered something indecipherable, a question – what? how? when? *what?* – and watched

Chie's pale face flush crimson suddenly as if the speaking of those words had given heat to her grief.

Since that news, they find themselves looking down at earth as they circle their way around it (meanderingly it seems, though that couldn't be less true), and there's that word: mother mother mother mother. Chie's only mother now is that rolling, glowing ball that throws itself involuntarily around the sun once a year. Chie has been made an orphan, her father dead a decade. That ball is the only thing she can point to now that has given her life. There's no life without it. Without that planet there's no life. Obvious.

Think a new thought, they sometimes tell themselves. The thoughts you have in orbit are so grandiose and old. Think a new one, a completely fresh unthought one.

But there are no new thoughts. They're just old thoughts born into new moments – and in these moments is the thought: without that earth we are all finished. We couldn't survive a second without its grace, we are sailors on a ship on a deep, dark unswimmable sea.

None of them knows what to say to Chie, what consolation you can offer to someone who suffers the shock of bereavement while in orbit. You must want surely to get home, and say some sort of goodbye. No need to speak; you only have to look out through the window at a radiance doubling and redoubling. The earth, from here, is like heaven. It flows with colour. A burst of hopeful colour. When we're on that planet we look up and think heaven is elsewhere, but here is what the astronauts and cosmonauts sometimes think: maybe all of us born to it have already died and are in an afterlife. If we must go to an improbable, hard-to-believe-in place when we die, that glassy, distant orb with its beautiful lonely light shows could well be it.

Orbit 1, into orbit 2

You aren't even the farthest-flung humans now, says ground control. How does that feel?

For today a crew of four is on its way to the moon and has just surpassed the space station's shallow orbiting distance of two hundred and fifty miles above the planet. The lunar astronauts are catapulted past them in a five-billion-dollar blaze of suited-booted glory.

For the first time ever you've been overtaken, say ground crews. You're yesterday's news, they joke, and Pietro jokes back that better yesterday's news than tomorrow's, if they know what he means. If you're an astronaut you'd rather not ever be news. And here's the thing, thinks Chie, her mother's down there on that earth. Everything that's left of her mother's down there. Better to be lassoing it like this than watching it disappear in the rear-view mirror. Anton just looks out of the space-viewing portal to where he knows the constellations of Pegasus and Andromeda to be, though his vision can't readily sift them out among the millions of stars.

He's tired. Doesn't sleep that well up here, mind too constantly jet-lagged and staggered. There's Saturn, there's
the aeroplane shape of Aquila. The moon's a stone's
throw. One day, he thinks, he'll get there.

Mornings, a surge of sweat and breath and effort, weights
and bike and treadmill, the two hours a day when their
bodies are not suspended and are instead forced to comply
with gravity. In the Russian segment of the craft, Anton
on the bike shaking off what sleep he had, Roman on
the treadmill. Three modules away in the non-Russian
segment there's Nell on the bench press watching her
muscles work under a sheen of sweat while the pistons
and flywheel simulate gravity. Her lean, firm limbs have
no definition, no matter how you push and press and pedal
for these two hours in the gym still there are twenty-two
more hours every day in which the body has no force
to work against. Next to her Pietro is harnessed to the
US treadmill, listening to Duke Ellington with his eyes
closed; here in his head are the wild mint meadows of
Emilia-Romagna. Chie, in the next module, on the bike
with her teeth clenched and the resistance up high, counting out the cadence of her pedalling.

   Up here in microgravity you're a seabird on a warm
day drifting, just drifting. What use are biceps, calves,

strong shin bones; what use muscle mass? Legs are a thing of the past. But every day the six of them have to fight this urge to dissipate. They retreat inside their headphones and press weights and cycle nowhere at twenty-three times the speed of sound on a bike that has no seat or handlebars, just a set of pedals attached to a rig, and run eight miles inside a slick metal module with a close-up view of a turning planet.

Sometimes they wish for a cold stiff wind, blustery rain, autumn leaves, reddened fingers, muddy legs, a curious dog, a startled rabbit, a leaping sudden deer, a puddle in a pothole, soaked feet, a slight hill, a fellow runner, a shaft of sun. Sometimes they just succumb to the uneventful windless humming of their sealed spacecraft. While they run, while they cycle, while they push and press, the continents and oceans fall away beneath – the lavender Arctic, the eastern tip of Russia vanishing behind, storms strengthening over the Pacific, the desert- and mountain-creased morning deserts of Chad, southern Russia and Mongolia and the Pacific once more.

Anyone in Mongolia or those easternmost wilder-nesses of Russia, or anyone at least who knows about such things, would be aware that now, in their cold afternoon sky, higher than any aeroplane, a spacecraft is passing and that some human is up there hefting a lift-bar with her legs, willing her muscles not to give in to the seduction of weightlessness, nor her bones to birdness. Else that poor spacefarer will be in all kinds of trouble when she lands back on earth where legs, once more, are very much a thing. Without that hefting and sweating and pressing she would survive the blazing heat and tumble of her re-entry only to be pulled from her capsule and fold like a paper crane.

At some point in their stay in orbit there comes for each of them a powerful desire that sets in – a desire never to leave. A sudden ambushing by happiness. They find it everywhere, this happiness, springing forth from the blandest of places – from the experiment decks, from within the sachets of risotto and chicken cassoulet, from the panels of screens, switches and vents, from the brutally cramped titanium, Kevlar and steel tubes in which they're trapped, from the very floors which are walls and the walls which are ceilings and the ceilings which are floors. From the handholds which are foot-holds which chafe the toes. From the spacesuits, which wait in the airlocks somewhat macabre. Everything that speaks of being in space – which is everything – ambushes them with happiness, and it isn't so much that they don't want to go home but that home is an idea that has imploded – grown so big, so distended and full, that it's caved in on itself.

At first on their missions they each miss their families, sometimes so much that it seems to scrape out their insides; now, out of necessity, they've come to see that their family is this one here, these others who know the things they know and see the things they see, with whom they need no words of explanation. When they get back how will they even begin to say what happened to them, who and what they were? They want no view except this view from the window of the solar arrays as they taper into emptiness. No rivets in the entirety of the world will do except these rivets around the window frames. They want padded gangways for the rest of their lives. This continuous hum.

They feel space trying to rid them of the notion of days. It says: what's a day? They insist it's twenty-four hours and ground crews keep telling them so, but it takes their twenty-four hours and throws sixteen days and nights at them in return. They cling to their twenty-four-hour clock because it's all the feeble little time-bound body knows – sleep and bowels and all that is leashed to it. But the mind goes free within the first week. The mind is in a dayless freak zone, surfing earth's hurtling horizon. Day is here, and then they see night come upon them like the shadow of a cloud racing over a wheat field. Forty-five minutes later here comes day again, stampeding across the Pacific. Nothing is what they thought it was.

Now as they track south from eastern Russia diagonally across the Sea of Okhotsk, Japan appears in the mauve-grey sheen of mid-afternoon. Their pass intersects the narrow line of the Kuril Islands that tread a worn-out path between Japan and Russia. In this indistinct light the islands seem to Chie to be a trail of drying footprints. Her country is a ghost haunting the water. Her country is a dream she remembers once having. It lies slantwise and slight.

She looks out from the lab window as she towels herself off after exercise. Her weightless bobbing is steady and upright. If she could stay in orbit for the rest of her life all would be well. It's only when she goes back that her mother is dead; as in musical chairs when there's one fewer seat than there are humans who need it, but so long as the music plays the number of seats is immaterial and everyone is still in the game. You have to not stop. You have to keep moving. You have this glorious orbit and when you're orbiting you're impact-proof and nothing can touch you. When the planet is galloping through space and you gallop after it through light and dark with your time-drunk brain, nothing can end. There could be no end, there can be only circles.

Don't go back. Stay here ongoing. The creamy light off the ocean so exquisite; the gentle clouds rippling in tides. With a zoom lens the first fall of snow on the top of Mount Fuji, the silver bracelet of the Nagara River where she swam as a child. Just here, the perfect solar arrays drinking sun.

From the space station's distance mankind is a creature that comes out only at night. Mankind is the light of cities and the illuminated filament of roads. By day, it's gone. It hides in plain sight.

On this orbit, orbit two of today's sixteen, they can watch if ever they have such a stretch of time, and traverse the earth one whole round and see barely a trace of human or animal life.

Their transit approaches West Africa just as morning breaks. The vast spill of day blots out every obvious human landmark to the naked eye. They pass central Africa, the Caucasus and Caspian Sea, southern Russia, Mongolia, eastern China, the north of Japan in the blanching light. By the time night comes in the Western Pacific there's no land in sight, no cities to proclaim mankind. On this orbit the entire night-pass is oceanic and black, stealing down the mid-Pacific between New Zealand and South America, brushing the tip of Patagonia and back up to Africa, and just as the ocean runs out and the coasts of Liberia and Ghana and Sierra Leone creep up, sunrise blasts open the dark and daytime floods in, the entire northern hemisphere once again luminous and humanless. Seas, lakes, plains, deserts, mountains, estuaries, deltas, forests and ice floes.

As they orbit they might as well be intergalactic travellers chancing upon a virgin frontier. *It seems uninhabited Captain*, they say when they glance out before breakfast. *We believe it could be the remnants of a collapsed civilisation. Prepare the thrusters for landing.*

Orbit 3, ascending

Why couldn't a spaceship be decked out like an old farm-house, with flowery wallpaper and oak beams – fake oak beams, says Pietro at breakfast. Lightweight non-flammable ones. And tatty armchairs and all these things. Like an old Italian farmhouse. Or an English one.

At which everybody looks at Nell, who is English, and who shrugs and digs about in her sachet of *perlovka*, the pearl-barley porridge Roman and Anton let her take from the Russian food stores; she stirs the syrup around.

Or like an old Japanese house, says Chie. Much better – lighter, less stuff.

I'd go for that, says Shaun, who is floating above them like an angel. He cocks a teaspoon at Chie as if a thought has just grabbed him. I went to an awesome Japanese house once, in Hiroshima, he says. A B&B type thing, run by American Christians.

You American Christians get everywhere, Chie says, pincering a piece of salmon with her chopsticks.

Yep, you leave the surface of the earth and you still can't shake us.

We'll shake you soon, says Roman.

Ah, but you'll be going back to earth and that's our breeding ground, Shaun replies, and looks around, nodding. I could get to like this place done out as an old Japanese house.

Pietro finishes his cereal and secures his spoon to the magnetised tray. Do you know what I'll look forward to getting back to, when the time comes? he says. Things I don't need, that's what. Pointlessness. Some pointless ornament on a shelf. A *rug*.

Roman laughs. Not alcohol or sex or – just a rug.

I didn't say what I'd *do* on the rug.

True, Anton says. You did not, and don't please.

What would you do? Nell asks.

Chie winks. Yes, Pietro, what would you do?

Lie there, Pietro says. And dream of space.

Day comes at them in a barrage.

Pietro will go and monitor his microbes that tell them something more about the viruses, funguses and bacteria that are present on the craft. Chie will continue growing her protein crystals, and attach herself to the MRI to have one of many routine brain scans that show the impact of microgravity on their neural functioning. Shaun will monitor his thale cress to see what happens to plant roots when they lack the gravity and light to know when and how to grow. Chie and Nell will check the well-being of and collect data for their forty resident mice who are enlightening them about muscle wastage in space, and later Shaun and Nell will conduct experiments on flammability. Roman and Anton will service the Russian oxygen generator and culture heart cells. Anton will water his cabbages and his dwarf wheat. They will all report on whether they have headaches and where in the head and how acute. They will all at some point take their cameras to the earth-viewing windows and photograph each of the locations on the list they've been given, in particular those Of Extra-Special Interest. They will: change the smoke detectors, change out the Water Resupply Tank in slot 2 and install a new tank in slot 3 of the Water Storage System, clean the bathroom and kitchen, fix the toilet-that-always-breaks. Their day is mapped by acronyms, MOP, MPC, PGP, RR, MRI, CEO, OESI, WRT for WSS, T-T-A-B.

Today there is one item on the Of Extra-Special Interest list above all others, the typhoon moving over the

Western Pacific towards Indonesia and the Philippines, which seems suddenly to have gathered force. Not visible yet on their current path, but in two more orbits they'll have shifted west and caught up with it. Can they take photographs and videos, can they confirm satellite images, can they comment on its size and speed? All of which they're used to doing, being weathermen and women, early warning systems. They note the orbits that will cross the typhoon's path – this morning's orbits four, five and six going south, and tonight's orbits thirteen and fourteen going north, though they'll be back in bed by the time those come.

Earlier that morning Nell had an email from her brother saying he was unwell with the flu, and that struck her, how long it has been since she was ill – she feels in space as though her body is young again and there are no aches or pains, except for the space headaches they all get – even those are rare for her. Something about having your weight taken off you, having no pressure on your joints and no pressure on your mind – no choices. Your days are laid out minute by minute in a schedule. You do someone else's bidding and you go to bed early and usually exhausted and you get up early and start again and the only decision to be made is what to eat, and that too is limited.

In his email her brother said in half jest that he hates being ill alone and that it must be nice to be with five others all the time, your *floating family*, he called it. Up here, *nice* feels such an alien word. It's brutal, inhuman, overwhelming, lonely, extraordinary and magnificent. There isn't one single thing that is nice. She went to put that thought into words for her brother but it felt like she was making an argument or trying to outdo or undermine what he'd told her, so she wrote only to send love and attached a photo of the Severn Estuary at sunrise, one of the moon, one of Chie and Anton at the observation windows. She finds she often struggles for things to tell people at home, because the small things are too mundane and the rest is too astounding and there seems to be nothing in between, none of the usual gossip, the he-said-she-said, the ups and downs; there is a lot of round and round. There's a lot of contemplation of how it's possible to get nowhere very fast.

This is a strange thing, it seems to her. All your dreams of adventure and freedom and discovery culminate in the aspiration to become an astronaut, and then you get up here and you are trapped, and spend your days packing and unpacking things, and fiddle in a laboratory with pea shoots and cotton roots, and go nowhere but round and round with the same old thoughts going round and round with you.

This isn't a complaint. God, no, this isn't a complaint.

Don't encroach, is their unspoken rule. Little enough space and privacy as it is, all of them stuck here together in each other's pockets breathing each other's overused air for months on end. Don't cross the rubicon into one another's internal lives.

There is that idea of a *floating family*, but in some ways they're not really a family at all – they're both much more and much less than that. They're everything to each other for this short stretch of time because they're all there is. They're companions, colleagues, mentors, doctors, dentists, hairdressers. On spacewalks, launches, re-entry, in emergencies, they're each other's lifelines. They are each to the other a representative of the human race – they each have to suffice for billions of people. They have to make do in lieu of every earthly thing – families, animals, weather, sex, water, trees. Walking. Some days they just want to *walk*, or lie down. When they miss people and things, when earth feels so far away that depression washes over them for days and even the view of the sun setting over the Arctic isn't enough to lift them, then they have to be able to see the face of one of the others on board and find something there that keeps them going. Some solace. They don't always. Nell might look at Shaun some days and resent him for failing to be her husband. Anton will wake resentful because none of these people is his daughter or son or anyone or anything he loves. This is the way it goes – and then another day they look into the face of one of those five people and there in their way of smiling or concentrating or eating is everything and everyone they've ever loved, all of it, just there, and humanity, in coming down in its essence to this handful of people, is no longer a species of confounding difference and distance but a near and graspable thing.

They have talked before about a feeling they often have, a feeling of merging. That they are not quite distinct from one another, nor from the spaceship. Whatever they were before they came here, whatever their differences in training or background, in motive or character, whatever country they hail from and however their nations clash, they are equalised here by the delicate might of their spaceship. They are a choreographing of movements and functions of the ship's body as it enacts its perfect choreography of the planet. Anton – quiet, and dry in his humour, sentimental, crying openly at films, at scenes outside the window – Anton the space-ship's heart. Pietro its mind, Roman (the current commander, dextrous and capable, able to fix anything, control the robotic arm with millimetre precision, wire the most complex circuit board) its hands, Shaun its soul (Shaun there to convince them all that they have souls), Chie (methodical, fair, wise, not-quite definable or pin-downable) its conscience, Nell (with her eight-litre diving lungs) its breath.

Then they agree that it's idiotic, this metaphor. Nonsensical. But unshakeable all the same. There's something about hurtling in low earth orbit that makes them think this way, as a unit, where the unit itself, their sprawling ship, becomes alive and part of them. They thought they'd find it precarious, this fact of living in a complex life-support machine and the prospect that it could, instantaneously, all end – a failure in any part of the machine. A fire, an ammonia leak, radiation, a meteor strike. And in moments they do – but generally not so, and anyway, all beings are living in life-support machines commonly called bodies and all of these will fail eventually. This one, precarious though it surely is, is limited to its orbiting groove, a place of few surprises, all unforeseens foreseen – watched twenty-four seven, assiduously monitored, obsessively repaired, comprehensively alarmed, thoughtfully padded, few sharp objects, no trip hazards, nothing to fall off. Not the multiple perils of earthly freedom where you roam about quite unmonitored, quite unbounded, beset by ledges and heights and roads and guns and mosquitoes and contagion and crevasses and the hapless criss-cross of eight million species all vying to survive.

The surprising thought occurs to them sometimes: they are encapsulated, a submarine moving alone through the vacuum depths, and when they leave it they will feel less safe. They will reappear on the earth's surface as strangers of a kind. Aliens learning a mad new world.

Orbit 3, descending

Think of a house. A wooden house on a Japanese island near the sea, with sliding paper doors wide to the garden and tatami floors sun-blanched and threadbare. Imagine a butterfly on the tap at the kitchen sink, a dragonfly on the folded futon, a spider inside a slipper in the front porch.

Think of a wooden house that's worn, all its wood smooth to the touch. Worn by the humidity and heat and snow, and dishevelled by small earthquakes. Then imagine a youngish man and woman bent over their vegetable patch outside while the lead weight of the August sky bears down. Pumpkins growing, lots of them, as big as the moon looks in its summer fullness, and nothing but the sound of the sea. No, nothing but the sound of cicadas, crickets, bullfrogs, the tear-tear of the woman's hands at weeds, the tap-tap of the man's brisk voice between bouts of digging, and the sea.

Then track the seasons through many years, and the man is manoeuvring his creaking parched self into a pair of trousers and wondering how he seems to have aged so much more than his wife who is still wiry-spry and steps out with a spring. He can't muster much saliva any more and nobody told him that old age would be quite so dry, his skin, mouth and eyes – his nose with nothing much left to blow (he blows it anyway, all the time). What a stupefyingly ill-prepared thing his body is to dry up. Like a leaf, you might think, but a dry leaf falls from the branch and he isn't ready to go. Gets up at dawn and stands at the dyke where the bullfrogs belch and digs his toes in.

Track the seasons another half-year and the man is gone. The woman tends her days alone. The years pass, ten of them, and a warm autumn comes with a few last pumpkins on sprawling stems. Mildew on the stems and the wooden door frame and the wooden step; a morning dampness to the paper screens. The most beautiful evening skies of late. The woman lies on one of the narrow steps, she is narrow too, a broomstick is how she sees herself. All this woodenness around her and no human beings, so she has turned to wood so as not to be outdone.

You know sometimes when a day is your last and she would never in a million years lie outside like this in the early evening on her step in some gesture of late abandon, minor rebellion – a tough old broomstick, she.

Dislikes nonsense. But her blood has slowed and everything has slowed. She has not felt well these last weeks.
She has looked to see the moving point of light in the
sky that, since her husband's death, has made nearly
sixty thousand orbits of the earth and has thought she
would try to wait another month for her daughter to
come back. But since when did death wait, and what
sort of a homecoming would it be anyway? To die on
her daughter's arrival on earth. Her extremities feel
suddenly hot, like her heart is trying to send the blood
away from itself. Let me rest, her heart is saying. She
hears a cicada, never before would you hear a cicada
this late in the year, it's so warm now all the time that
they don't know when to die. It sounds like one lone
long-lingering male, and perhaps she would linger that
long if she'd been buried underground for fifteen years
awaiting her turn to mate, but now his call isn't one
of mating but of solitude, a leave-me-be, just that one
call in the quiet dusk.

Track the days forward one and then two and then
three and then four, and the body has been taken from
the step and the house is deserted. From that invisible
light in the dull evening sky, where the woman's daughter is stationed, Asia slides away to the starboard side.
Shikoku and Kyushu pass beneath, and everything else

is ocean; the same ocean that raids the shore by the
wooden house, getting closer to the garden this last decade, where the pumpkins are starting to soften. Then
the last of Asia is gone to the west and the aft and there's
nothing at all except the deep trench of the Pacific, and
their orbit presses south-east for thousands of empty
bright miles.

There, in that emptiness, the typhoon is organising. For
the last twenty-four hours it's been shifting west, by now
past the Marshall Islands, that fragile tracery of sinking
lands so piecemeal and storm-worn. First some clumping
of high drifting cloud, the clouds congregating from
all directions, denser and darker; not one storm but a
collision of several, and it's clear now that the cloud is
muscling and spiralling into what could be at the very
least a Category Four typhoon.

Take as many photographs as you can, the crew is
told, and they do, their long lenses against the glass,
shutters stuttering, seeing only the eastern arm of the
storm so far, off to starboard where it wraps itself against
the earth's horizon in flocks of spun grey; seeing in detail what nobody on earth can see – how the clouds are
ordering themselves anticlockwise, a whipped-up rowdy
march. Sunlight rebounds off the cloud's milky cover

and the earth has the eerie pearl-glow of an eye shot with cataracts. It seems to fix them with an unsteady stare.

How wired and wakeful the earth seems suddenly. It's not one of the regular typhoons that haphazardly assault these parts of the world, they agree. They can't see it all, but it's bigger than projections had previously thought, and moving faster. They send their images, the latitudes and longitudes. They are like fortune tellers, the crew. Fortune tellers who can see and tell the future but do nothing to change or stop it. Soon their orbit will descend away to the east and south and no matter how they crane their necks backward at the earth-viewing windows the typhoon will roll out of sight and their vigil will end and darkness will hit them at speed.

They have no power – they have only their cameras and a privileged anxious view of its building magnificence. They watch it come.

Orbit 4, ascending

In the new morning of today's fourth earth orbit the Saharan dust sweeps to the sea in hundred-mile ribbons. Hazy pale green shimmering sea, hazy tangerine land. This is Africa chiming with light. You can almost hear it, this light, from inside the craft. Gran Canaria's steep radial gorges pile the island up like a sandcastle hastily built, and when the Atlas Mountains announce the end of the desert, clouds appear in the shape of a shark whose tail flips at the southern coast of Spain, whose fin-tip nudges the southern Alps, whose nose will dive any moment into the Mediterranean. Albania and Montenegro are velvet soft with mountain.

Where do the boundaries sit, Shaun thinks as he moves past the window. He tries to place it all – Montenegro, Serbia, Hungary, Romania, he can never remember the exact arrangement. You could spend your days, your entire orbiting life, with your Rand McNally Atlas and your maps of the stars. You could do no work whatsoever. You could abandon it all, just to look. You

could know the earth inside out, in its little hollow of
space. You could never really comprehend the stars, but
the earth you could know in the way you know another
person, in the way he came quite studiedly and deter-
minedly to know his wife. With a yearning that's hungry
and selfish. He wishes to know it, inch by inch.

In microgravity their arteries are thickening and stiff-
ening and the muscle of the heart weakening and
shrinking. Those hearts, so inflated with ecstasy at the
spectacle of space, are at the same time withered by it.
And when heart cells are damaged or depleted they don't
renew too well, so here they are, their own tender hearts
waning and toughening while they try to preserve the
heart cells in their dishes.

In these dishes is humanity, Anton says to Roman in
the Russian lab. The two of them move humanity about
with their pipettes. The pink-purple-red configuration of
cells was once the skin taken from human volunteers,
the skin cells reverted back to stem cells, the stem cells
into heart cells. The skin samples were taken from people of different ages, backgrounds, races. This is quietly
astounding to Anton in a way it isn't to his lab-mate, who
treats them with a care free of reverence, the same care
he gives to electrical wiring. Whereas Anton's fingertips

seem actually to warm in the presence of the cells. To become almost too hot. All this various life with which he's been troublingly entrusted. Look Roman, he wants to say. What kind of absurd miracle is this? All of this? Roman doesn't seem troubled or humbled by it at all, or even thoughtful, he only says, I don't know what it is about the colours in these dishes that always makes me feel hungry. So the moment passes.

They watch these cells under the microscope and take images of them, and every five days they renew the medium they grow in. They keep them at thirty-seven degrees and at five per cent carbon and at ideal humidity and in perfect sterility, and when the resupply craft returns to earth in two weeks they'll stow them away, a cargo they must accept is more important to humanity than their lives themselves, which are nothing much all told.

Whatever is happening to these cells in their incubator is likely happening to their own, a fact they can't but acknowledge.

Not an encouraging thought, says Roman.

Well, Anton replies, and shrugs, and Roman too. What the shrug means is that they don't come into space to be encouraged. They come out of a drive for more, more of everything, more knowledge and humility.

Speed and stillness. Distance and closeness. More less, more more. And what they find is that they are small, no, nothing. They nurture a bunch of cells *in vitro* which they can see only under a microscope and they know that their being alive in this moment depends on cells just like these in their own puny pulsing hearts.

After six months in space they will, in technical terms, have aged 0.007 seconds less than someone on earth. But in other respects they'll have aged five or ten years more, and this is only in the ways they currently understand. They know that the vision can weaken and the bones deteriorate. Even with so much exercise still the muscles will atrophy. The blood will clot and the brain shift in its fluid. The spine lengthens, the T cells struggle to reproduce, kidney stones form. While they're here food tastes of little. Their sinuses are murder. Proprioception falters – it's hard to know where their body parts are without looking. They become misshapen bags of fluid, too much in the upper body and not enough lower down. Fluid gathers behind the eyeball and squashes the optic nerve. Sleep mutinies. Their gut microbiomes grow new bacteria. Their cancer risk increases.

Not encouraging thoughts, as Roman says. Anton asks him a while later if he worries about this.

No, he says. Never. And you?

Beneath them the South Pacific now passes in absolute night, an endless pit of black, and there is no planet, just the gentle green line of the atmosphere and numberless stars, astonishing solitude, everything so near and infinite.

No, Anton answers. Never.

Sometimes they look at the earth and could be tempted to roll back all they know to be true, and to believe instead that it sits, this planet, at the centre of everything. It seems so spectacular, so dignified and regal. They could still be led to believe that God himself had dropped it there, at the very centre of the waltzing universe, and they could forget all those truths men and women had uncovered (via a jerking and stuttering path of discovery followed by denial followed by discovery followed by cover-up) that the earth is a piddling speck at the centre of nothing. They could think: no negligible thing could shine so bright, no far-hurled nothingy satellite could bother itself with these shows of beauty, no paltry rock could arrange such intricacy as fungus and minds.

So they sometimes think it would be easier to unwind the heliocentric centuries and go back to the years of a divine and hulking earth around which all things orbited – the sun, the planets, the universe itself. You'd need far more distance from the earth than they have to find it insignificant and small; to really understand its cosmic place. Yet it's clearly not that kingly earth of old, a God-given clod too stout and stately to be able to move about the ballroom of space; no. Its beauty echoes – its beauty is its echoing, its ringing singing lightness. It's not peripheral and it's not the centre; it's not everything and it's not nothing, but it seems much more than something. It's made of rock but appears from here as gleam and ether, a nimble planet that moves three ways – in rotation on its axis, at a tilt on its axis, and around the sun. This planet that's been relegated out of the centre and into the sidelines – the thing that goes around rather than is gone around, except for by its knobble of moon. This thing that harbours we humans who polish the ever-larger lenses of our telescopes that tell us how ever-smaller we are. And we stand there gaping. And in time, we come to see that not only are we on the sidelines of the universe but that it's of a universe of sidelines, that there is no centre, just a giddy mass of waltzing things, and that perhaps the entirety of our understanding consists of an elaborate and ever-evolving knowledge of our own extraneousness, a bashing away of mankind's ego by the instruments of scientific enquiry until it is, that ego, a shattered edifice that lets light through.

They sail at their in-between distance of low earth orbit, their half-mast view. They think: maybe it's hard being human and maybe that's the problem. Maybe it's hard to shift from thinking your planet is safe at the centre of it all to knowing in fact it's a planet of normalish size and normalish mass rotating about an average star in a solar system of average everything in a galaxy of innumerably many, and that the whole thing is going to explode or collapse.

Maybe human civilisation is like a single life – we grow out of the royalty of childhood into supreme normality; we find out about our own unspecialness and in a flush of innocence we feel quite glad – if we're not special then we might not be alone. If there are who-knows-how-many solar systems just like ours, with who-knows-how-many planets, one of those planets is surely inhabited, and companionship is our consolation for being trivial. And so, in loneliness and curiosity and hope, humanity looks outwards and thinks they might be on Mars perhaps, the others, and sends out probes. But Mars appears to be a frozen desert of cracks and craters, so maybe in that case they're in the neighbouring solar system, or the neighbouring galaxy, or the one after that.

We send out the Voyager probes into interstellar space in a big-hearted fanciful spasm of hope. Two capsules from earth containing images and songs just waiting to be found in – who knows – tens or hundreds of thousands of years if all goes well. Otherwise millions or billions, or not at all. Meanwhile we begin to listen. We scan the reaches for radio waves. Nothing answers. We keep on scanning for decades and decades. Nothing answers. We make wishful and fearful projections through books, films and the like about how it might look, this alien life, when it finally makes contact. But it doesn't make contact and we suspect in truth that it never will. It's not even out there, we think. Why bother waiting when there's nothing there? And now maybe humankind is in the late smash-it-all-up teenage stage of self-harm and nihilism, because we didn't ask to be alive, we didn't ask to inherit an earth to look after, and we didn't ask to be so completely unjustly darkly alone.

Maybe one day we'll look in the mirror and be happy with the fair-to-middling upright ape that eyes us back, and we'll gather our breath and think: OK, we're alone, so be it. Maybe that day is coming soon. Maybe the whole nature of things is one of precariousness, of wobbling on a pinhead of being, of decentring ourselves inch by inch as we do in life, as we come to understand that the staggering extent of our own non-extent is a tumultuous and wave-tossed offering of peace.

Until then what can we do in our abandoned solitude but gaze at ourselves? Examine ourselves in endless
bouts of fascinated distraction, fall in love and in hate
with ourselves, make a theatre, myth and cult of ourselves. Because what else is there? To become superb in
our technology, knowledge and intellect, to itch with a
desire for fulfilment that we can't quite scratch; to look
to the void (which still isn't answering) and build space-
ships anyway, and make countless circlings of our lonely
planet, and little excursions to our lonely moon and
think thoughts like these in weightless bafflement and
routine awe. To turn back to the earth, which gleams
like a spotlit mirror in a pitch-dark room, and speak
into the fuzz of our radios to the only life that appears
to be there. Hello? *Konnichiwa, ciao, zdraste, bonjour,* do
you read me, hello?

Thousands of miles distant from their orbit and
around the earth's curve, in a beach hut near Cape
Canaveral, there are four beds which were, yesterday,
vacated by another set of astronauts. This time yesterday morning two women and two men were in their
last hour of sleep before an alarm sounded their day;
only 5 a.m. in Florida and their bellies were still full
of the barbecue they'd had the night before, burrowed

in sleep that was drugged and dreamless. They were out cold; they didn't dribble or snore or twitch or rouse.

When the moon had started to fade and the sleeping-pill paralysis had begun to ease, the two women and men had opened their eyes and thought: something happens today. Where am I? What is it that happens today? This anticipation, dormant in sleep, then instantly shrill. The moon, the moon – we go to the moon, Jesus-shit, we go to the moon. Their spacesuits and rocket awaited. Nothing would be the same for them again. But this time yesterday they'd not yet woken and were still in their beach-hut quarantine, the air around them reeking of sausage and ribs and flame-grilled corn. It had been well and good, their last supper, some normality to take their minds off it all. But the moon had gatecrashed. There it was, so small and far. Its cold hard light bore down and drove an axe through their appetites. A burger half-eaten, the ribs barely gnawed, zero-alcohol beer undrunk, a last-minute wobble, a pill taken, legs of jelly, a prayer muttered, and early to bed.

Over fifty years without a human foot on its back, our moon, and does it turn its bright side in longing to the earth in the hope of the humans' return? Does it, and all of the other moons and planets and solar systems and galaxies, yearn to be known? Late tomorrow, after fewer than three days travelling, these strange obsessed human creatures will be back on its powdered surface, these beings who insist on flying flags in a windless world, these single-minded marshmallow folk, bloated sailors of the sky, to find their flagstaffs toppled and their Stars and Stripes tattered. That's what happens when you're away for fifty years, things move on without you. So slept the four astronauts in the beach hut, knowing a new era would begin when they opened their eyes.

And now it's begun, that era, it's here. The astronauts left their beds yesterday morning, ate some breakfast and embarked on their exactly regimented day. The cleaners came in and, with a sense of ceremony, stripped the beds they'd left, and washed the dishes and cleaned out the barbecue. At five in the evening the rocket eventually launched. There were two full orbits they made of the earth last night before they propelled themselves clear, and now, with their launch fuel burned and their boosters jettisoned, they'll be reeling out in increments along a path of two hundred and fifty thousand miles whose every inch is mapped in numbers, and they'll go that way until tomorrow night when they reach the moon.

Last night the six astronauts here dug out the party things, blew up some balloons, hung out the birthday bunting, and prepared themselves as celebratory a meal as they could muster from the library of silver sachets – they found some chocolate puddings and peach cobblers and packets of custard. Roman hung up the little felt moon his son had given him and which had been one of the few things he'd brought with him to space. They felt elation mixed with angst mixed with envy mixed with pride which looped back to elation, and in the end they went to bed early as they always do. Because moon landing or not, there's an early morning. There's always, every day, an early morning.

And there's a backlash feeling, quiet and unshared but there in them all, of what has suddenly become their own mundaneness. The mundaneness of their earth-stuck orbit, bound for nowhere; their looping round and never *out*. Their loyal, monogamous circling which struck them last night as humbly beautiful. A sense of attention and servitude, a sort of worship. And though they looked out before going to bed, as if they might see those moon-bound astronauts sailing past, and though their sleep was restless with anticipation, it wasn't the moon that entered their dreams, but their own wild garden of space outside the spacecraft – the garden they'd all at some point walked in. And the ever-electric blue pull of the earth.

Irritating things:
   Tailgaters
   Tired children
   Wanting to go for a run
   Lumpy pillows
   Peeing in space when in a hurry
   Stuck zips
   Whispering people
   The Kennedys

Chie clips her lists to the storage pouches in her sleeping quarters, where she puts her keepsakes, her few personal effects; a small tube of skin emollient for the sore dryness that afflicts her hands, a black and white photograph of her young mother on the beach near their house, a poetry collection about Japanese mountains which her uncle sent up in the last crew package and which she has no time for at all. She tears out its blank pages at the back and on them she scrawls her lists in a loose and sketchy hand.

Reassuring things:
   The earth below
   Mugs with sturdy handles
   Trees

Wide stairways
Home-knits
Nell's singing
Strong knees
Pumpkins

Out there on the nadir of the craft is the unit that Pietro
and Nell installed on their spacewalk the week before, a
spectrometer that measures the radiance of the earth. It
sweeps a seventy-kilometre swathe of the planet as the
craft orbits, moving from continent to continent, north
and south, an obsessive eye watching, gathering, cali-
brating light.

Pietro has had other missions and other spacewalks
and run however many thousands of experiments in
his four-hundred-ish days in space, and there's a sense
of level-headed distance about it all, you run the experiment or you install the unit or you collect the data and
then you pass it on and move to the next. What are
you anyway as an astronaut but a conduit – you are
selected for your non-stick temperament, maybe one day
a robot could do your job and maybe it will; you have
to wonder. They do sometimes wonder. A robot has no
need for hydration, nutrients, excretion, sleep, a robot
has no irksome brain fluids or menstruation or libido or

taste buds. You don't have to fly fruit to it on a rocket or fill it with vitamins and antioxidants and sleeping pills and painkillers, nor build for it a toilet with funnels and pumps that requires a training course to use, nor a unit that recycles its urine into drinking water, since it has no urine and it needs no water and it wants and asks for nothing.

But what would it be to cast out into space creations that had no eyes to see it and no heart to fear or exult in it? For years an astronaut trains in pools and caves and submarines and simulators, every flaw or weakness located, tested and winnowed away until what's left is a near-perfect unflappable triangulation of brain, limbs and senses. For some it comes hard and for others more easily. For Pietro, more easily; he is a natural-born astronaut, he has an equilibrium that has been there since childhood, an extraordinary ease and presence of mind that made him bypass most of the shit-slinging tantrums of toddler-dom and rebellions of adolescence. A deep curiosity, a brain of ornate architecture, a focus, an optimism and a pragmatism; an astronaut to his bones before he even knew what an astronaut was. But a robot, no.

There in his chest is a heart that tilts and pitches. He can keep its beats slow and smooth, quell its habits of fear or panic or impulse, stop it yearning too much for home, curb its unhelpful states of abandon. Calm and steady, calm and steady. Metronome pacing out the breath. Yet still at times it tilts and pitches. It wants what it wants and hopes what it hopes and needs what it needs and loves what it loves. So strenuously unrobotic is the astronaut's heart that it leaves the earth's atmosphere and it presses out – gravity stops pressing in and the counterweight of the heart starts pressing out, as if suddenly aware it is part of an animal, alive and feeling. An animal that does not just bear witness, but loves what it witnesses.

And so Pietro thinks about the spectrometer out there, which will help ascertain if the earth is dimming. Since he and Nell installed it, he thinks about it each day when he wakes up, its lenses pointing three ways, to the earth, the sun and moon, measuring the light that is reflected off the earth's surface and the clouds. Whether the earth's surface is dimming because the particulates in the air from pollutants reflect the sun's light back into space, or brightening because the melting ice sheet and lessening high bright cloud mean that more of the sun's light is absorbed by the earth. Or both at once, and then to what effect? This complex system of energy exchange which determines the temperature of the planet.

He thinks about the latter – the prospect of the earth absorbing more light – less light reflected back into space. From here, looking down, what would it be to see a less radiant planet? On a day like this seeing, as he captures videos, its patterning of clouds and the wide spectrum of its oceans' blues in morning light, a hologram arising out of blackness. Radiance itself. What would it be to lose this? To starboard, the soft brushed nickel of the Mediterranean sheened by sun, the pleating and folding of the Dolomites and Alps, dark snowless peaks, indigo valleys, olive plains, the endless run of riverbeds, the tawny southern lands of his own country after a summer with no rain. Vesuvius just visible if you know where to look. Early October now, and still, he's told, no rain. And yet regardless the planet sings with light as if from its core, from the belly of itself, this great photogenic thing which he collects in his lens.

Eastern Europe slides past, and into Russia and over Mongolia and down through China, twenty minutes is all that takes, and he waits for the typhoon to come round. It's just there, he knows, beyond the planet's next bend, tucked on the other side of this bright blue curve, and his view of it will be full and almost directly above. Every day it surprises him. How unexpectedly strange it is for that spaceship of a planet to be sailing past his vision. Perhaps there is no other such observed object in the universe – who knows? It isn't just his eyes or those of the rest of crew observing it, not just the lenses of the spectrometer, but the other earth-viewing imagers attached to the station and thousands of satellites swarming and buzzing in high and low orbit, billions of radio waves transmitted and received.

Here he is now, a non-robot with a camera and a pair of twenty-twenty eyes and a heart pitching forwards, tripping up, at the earth's singularity. It bangs against his ribs as he films.

Orbit 4, descending

Their hands are in sealed experiment boxes or assembling or disassembling ruggedised units or refilling the auto-release food pouches in the modules of mice, their feet are in tethers at their workstations, their screwdrivers and spanners and scissors and pencils are drifting here and there about their heads and shoulders, a pair of tweezers breaks loose and sails towards the air vents which, in their imperceptible sucking, are the resting place of all lost things.

They descend past Shanghai, which by day is an unpeopled coast on the edge of a continent of every conceivable hue. Their fourth earth orbit of the waking day, and though their orbital path is in an eastward direction, all the same with each full transit their path shifts west because of the rotation of the earth, so that they – like the typhoon – move steadily inwards, off the Pacific, toward Malaysia and the Philippines, and the typhoon hustles in behind.

They stop whatever they're doing and take up their cameras. The clack of multiple shutters, the whir of lenses, the white soles of socks pitched up into the air while the crew congregate at earth-viewing windows butting gently against the bulletproof glass, taken aback by what they see. What they see is an unbroken vista of typhoon and a deep sucking well at its centre. A planet made entirely of spinning cloud.

On the ground people are told to evacuate. Images from space coming through, confirming what the eddying birds and running goats already seem to know, which is that this typhoon has found fuel enough to spread itself three hundred miles wide at a pressing speed. To all in the Philippines: get out or hunker down. To those on the tiny eastern islands, just get out. To one particular fisherman and his family, Pietro thinks, get out now, get out yesterday. But get out where? And how? And for the fisherman there's this protective urge not to leave your things, they being the few things you still have after the last typhoon and the one before that and the one before that. There are maybe twelve hours before it hits, and you are on an island that's off an island that's in the ocean, hopelessly low-lying. So all you can do is lie low hopelessly. You survived all the others. You have a house made of tin, cardboard, hardboard and sticks, and these days the typhoons are so frequent and huge that there's no point in building something better, it's easier to have nothing much to lose than to keep losing something.

So you stay. And you look up to the restless night sky where your unlikely astronaut friend spends his days, and emails you crazy photos of Samar, your island, in its turquoise seas. He would tell you to leave. Any minute now you'll look at your phone and there'll be a message from him telling you to leave. He'll tell you he can get someone to arrange it if need be, get you a flight.

Your wife says guardedly, *he is a kind man*, and this is true. The kindest of men. Sends you money each month for your children's school and has met you only that once, he on a diving trip (his honeymoon of all things) and you on your fishing boat. You'd dropped your line-cutting knife and it sank in a moment, cost you ten dollars that knife and was good and sharp. Then up surfaced the astronaut and his wife who'd been diving among shoals a dolphin-leap away, and they saw you peering over the edge of your boat. Down they went for fifteen minutes and refused to come up until they'd found your knife, flatly refused. It's alright, you'd said, by way of a raised hand, don't bother. But they bothered, and found it by some miracle wedged between rocks twenty-five metres down.

An astronaut and a fisherman. What a collision of worlds. He came to dinner with his wife and charmed your children and cast a spell of wonder on your card-board house as if he'd dropped in that afternoon from space itself, and though your wife's natural suspicions never quite eased she is mostly won over. Even the photo he took of you all has a spell of wonder – your wife slender-faced and rueful, you, yourself, intense and lion-like, the four children (sitting, standing, surprised, suspicious, serene, grinning, clinging) a collective of tumbled beauty – it made you notice as if for the first time quite how beautiful your children are.

You take the photograph now in your hand. If you were all going to flee from the storm this is the one thing you'd take, the astronaut's photo. But you are not going to flee. Flee to where? It isn't like that. You have your life and it can't be moved.

Up ahead is the Terminator, that sharp boundary line between day and night that falls across the full girth of the planet. It slices Papua New Guinea in two. This half is daylight, that half dark.

The island's day-lit half lies lush and dragon-like, its mountains mythical in the long last light, its coasts outlined by bioluminescent shores. Its dark half is a shadow on royal blue water. An electric light or two on the coast. The craft slides south-east into the thick of dark, the Solomon Islands, Vanuatu, Fiji, flecks of pale gold. Bowing away to starboard Canberra, Sydney and Brisbane in delicate brocade, then very much nothing save for the shuttle-woven tip of New Zealand which punctuates briefly the southern seas.

At this time of year there are fewer than six hours of absolute night over these more northerly regions of Antarctica, and the rest is day and shades of twilight. Now is that short steep night. In an Antarctic research base some migration biologists have just set up camp for the annual arrival of Arctic terns. They'll have flown pole-to-pole, these scant little birds. They'll have digested some of their internal organs to become long-distance athletes and travel some ten thousand miles. The beginning of October now, the Antarctic breaking free of what has been a long tenacious dusk, krill teeming below the ice. And those biologists will wait until bolts of white appear and the sky is filled with the sharp kip and caw of a coming flock. But now in the narrow interval of darkness the biologists come out to see something else. They don't

even need to look up to know it's there. Around their
base is a ring of green. The Martians are coming, they
say. They stamp their feet on the lunar-like snowfield
while red light splits open the Milky Way.

From up here in space where Roman glances out in
passing through the dome of windows, the view is at first
indistinct. It takes a moment to orientate. An expanse
of wintry nothingness, pearly cloud cover, and then
the familiar gleam of ice-sheet sloping off the Antarctic
Circle. Starboard, the Seven Sisters audaciously bright.
Sometimes there are urges to see a particular thing – the
Pyramids or the New Zealand fjords or a desert of sand
dunes that are bright orange and entirely abstract and
which the eye can't fathom – the image could just as
easily be a close-up of one of the heart cells they have
in their Petri dishes. Sometimes they want to see the
theatrics, the opera, the earth's atmosphere, airglow,
and sometimes it's the smallest things, the lights of fishing boats off the coast of Malaysia dotted starlike in the
black ocean. But now Roman can begin to see what he
suspected was there, a thing they all know, with a kind
of sixth sense, is there – the flexing, morphing green
and red of the auroras which snake around the inside of
the atmosphere fretful and magnificent like something
trapped.

Nell, he says, come quick. Nell, who is passing through the module, swims up into the dome. The two of them treading air in their lookout.

The airglow is dusty greenish yellow. Beneath it in the gap between atmosphere and earth is a fuzz of neon which starts to stir. It ripples, spills, it's smoke that pours across the face of the planet; the ice is green, the underside of the spacecraft an alien pall. The light gains edges and limbs; folds and opens. Strains against the inside of the atmosphere, writhes and flexes. Sends up plumes. Fluoresces and brightens. Detonates then in towers of light. Erupts clean through the atmosphere and puts up towers two hundred miles high. At the top of the towers is a swathe of magenta that obscures the stars, and across the globe a shimmering hum of rolling light, of flickering, quavering, flooding light, and the depth of space is mapped in light. Here the flowing, flooding green, there the snaking blades of neon, there the vertical columns of red, there the comets blazing by, there the close stars that seem to turn, there the far stars fixed in the heavens, beyond them the specks that can barely be seen.

By now Shaun and Chie have come, and Anton is at the window in the Russian module, and Pietro in the lab, the six of them drawn moth-like. The orbit rounds out above the Antarctic and begins its ascent towards the north. It leaves waves of aurora in its wake. The towers collapsing as if exhausted, twitches of green on the magnetic field. The South Pole recedes behind.

Roman's face is like that of a child. *Ofiget*, he murmurs. A *wow* snatched from the back of the throat. *Sugoii*, Chie replies, and Nell echoes it. *Remember* this, each of them thinks. Remember this.

Orbit 5, ascending

A fortnight or so ago, Anton had a dream about the imminent moon landing. In fact he had two dreams in two consecutive nights, both very similar (which is typical of his brain, to make technical repeats of the same dream as if to test its efficiency). It isn't that, being a cosmonaut, he normally dreams of the moon or space – on the contrary, being a cosmonaut he normally has very practical dreams about how to use a wrench to get himself out of the small window of a room on fire. Training dreams. But lately his nights are flooded with images, his dreams odd and wistful as if they are not really his but someone else's. And now this repeated one, no doubt because of those astronauts who left Cape Canaveral yesterday. He dreamed – of all things, of all damned American things – of the infamous image taken by Michael Collins during the first successful moon mission, back in 1969: the photograph of the lunar module leaving the moon's surface, and of the earth beyond.

No Russian mind should be steeped in these thoughts. There is no talk of it on their side and the silence is wholly begrudging – the thirteenth, fourteenth, fifteenth and sixteenth Americans to soon land on the moon's hallowed dusted crust, and yet still not a single Russian boot. Not one. Not a single Russian flag. No Russian brain should be dreaming about it, not this moon landing and not the first or the second or the third or fourth or the fifth or the sixth, but how do you stop your dreams?

In the photograph Collins took, there's the lunar module carrying Armstrong and Aldrin, just behind them the moon, and some two hundred and fifty thousand miles beyond that the earth, a blue half-sphere hanging in all blackness and bearing mankind. Michael Collins is the only human being not in that photograph, it is said, and this has always been a source of great enchantment. Every single other person currently in existence, to mankind's knowledge, is contained in that image; only one is missing, he who made the image.

Anton has never really understood that claim, or at least the enchantment of it. What of all the people on the other side of the earth that the camera can't see, and everybody in the southern hemisphere which is in night and gulped up by the darkness of space? Are they in the

photograph? In truth, nobody is in that photograph, nobody can be seen. Everybody is invisible – Armstrong and
Aldrin inside the lunar module, humankind unseen on a
planet that could easily, from this view, be uninhabited.
The strongest, most deducible proof of life in the photograph is the photographer himself – his eye at the view-
finder, the warm press of his finger on the shutter release.
In that sense, the more enchanting thing about Collins's
image is that, in the moment of taking the photograph,
he is really the *only* human presence it contains.

He imagines his father being very put out by this – that
the only human presence in that photograph, the only
life form in the universe, is American. He remembers
then how his father would tell him stories about Russian
moon landings, looping, detailed, extravagant tales that
he assumed, because his father told them, were true,
but which of course were fables. How powerfully did
those fables impact him. When he asked his father if
he, when he grew up, could be the next Russian to go
to the moon, his father said yes, he could, he would, it
was written in the stars. That on the moon's surface, by
the Russian flag, was a little box of Korovka, the milky
sweet he liked, left by the last visiting cosmonaut. That
the box had his name on, that he would one day eat
those Korovka.

He can't remember exactly when he realised that none of this was true – that no Russian had been to the moon, that there was no flag and no Korovka. Nor can he remember when he decided that, nevertheless, he would make one part of his father's stories true: he himself would go there. He told his wife that he would. He told her with utmost certainty and with pre-emptive pride and a swelling sense of national and personal and husbandly and later fatherly duty; he would go there, the first Russian, but not the last. Many years ago that was, that he told her all this.

In the first dream he had a fortnight ago he was simply looking at the photograph – or, the image in the photograph was his reality, as if he were Collins, and he was drifting out alone, the only man in the universe. In the second dream it was the same drifting, the same calm loneliness, and then he could hear something that became a faint murmur, the bubbling murmur of thousands or millions of voices, and when he listened in the earth zoomed closer and the voices clamoured and became one, which was his own. He saw himself, or perhaps not – he saw his voice, or *was* his voice – standing on the very surface of the earth looking out into space and to the moon, which was extremely distant, the size of a piece of grit – and he was shouting up at his wife who was now behind the lens of the camera somewhere on or near this distant moon. And of course she couldn't hear him, but somehow he knew she could see him through the camera lens, shouting and gesturing, as if to be rescued, or to effect rescue; he wasn't sure which.

Nell wants sometimes to ask Shaun how it is he can be an astronaut and believe in God, a Creationist God that is, but she knows what his answer would be. He'd ask how it is she can be an astronaut and not believe in God. They'd draw a blank. She'd point out of the port and starboard windows where the darkness is endless and ferocious. Where solar systems and galaxies are violently scattered. Where the field of view is so deep and multi-dimensional that the warp of space-time is something you can almost see. Look, she'd say. What made that but some heedless hurling beautiful force?

And Shaun would point out of the port and starboard windows where the darkness is endless and ferocious, at exactly the same violently scattered solar systems and galaxies and at the same deep and multidimensional field of view warped with space-time, and he would say: what made that but some heed*ful* hurling beautiful force?

Is that all the difference there is between their views, then – a bit of heed? Is Shaun's universe just the same

as hers but made with care, to a design? Hers an occurrence of nature and his an artwork? The difference
seems both trivial and insurmountable. She remembers
walking around a wood with her father one winter's day
when she was nine or ten and there was a full-size tree
that they almost walked straight past until they realised
it was man-made, it was a sculpture made from tens of
thousands of sticks glued together, woven to form the appearance of knots and bark and boles and branches. You
couldn't tell it apart from the other bare, wintry trees,
except that once you knew it was an artwork it pulsed
with a different energy, a different atmosphere. This
feels to her what separates her universe and Shaun's – a
tree made by the hand of nature, and a tree made by the
hand of an artist. It's barely any difference at all, and the
profoundest difference in the world.

But she doesn't ask him about any of this, and when
they're at lunch, just the two of them, Shaun says quite
suddenly, I watched the first moon landing with my father and uncle, one Sunday afternoon, a recording my
father had. And do you know what?

He hovers at the galley table with his fork plunging
toward a sachet of steak brisket, but halted mid-thought,
his fork arrested.

It was an event, he says, a coming of age, I was ten or eleven and it was the first thing I did with my father and uncle like that, where they seemed to be treating me as one of them. I didn't like it. That's the truth, I didn't like it.

There is Nell looking perpetually startled, her short hair and the way it stands as if some current runs through it, the puffy cheeks of the gravity-less. She cuts the top off a sachet of risotto which isn't as heated through as it could be, but there it is, she's hungry. As she eats she hangs like a seahorse, never quite still, and Shaun hangs opposite, never quite still. The faint billow of their clothes above the skin.

Before that, he says, I'd read all the space books as kids do, the books about the Shuttle programme, and I had posters on my walls of *Apollo* and *Discovery* and *Atlantis*. It was a dream I guess. But the day I watched a video of the first moon landing with my father and uncle, well, it was my father's face. He seemed to be full of this wanting, him and my uncle, like it made their own lives feel both empty and full at once. I didn't like it. It put me off. To think of my dad's face all hungry and lacking.

Nell thinks she knows it, that look, a look men get watching sports, football, say, in support of a team that affirms them by winning and then straight away negates them, because the glory belongs to the team, not the man sitting on the sofa who will never, now, be on a team like that.

Shaun has stopped eating, he lets his fork float and catches it, lets it float and catches it again.

And I thought that day, he says, I remember thinking – who'd want to be an astronaut? It seemed kind of crass to me suddenly, like they were projections of all the sad frustrated men of America.

Fantasies, Nell says.

Fantasies, Shaun says.

Nell nods. And Shaun laughs, as though to say, And now look at us.

I think, Nell says, when I watched the *Challenger* launch as a child, that was it for me. It wasn't the moon landings, it was *Challenger*. I realised space is real, space flight is real, a thing real people do, die doing. Real people, like me, could actually do it, and if I died doing it that would be OK, I could die that way. And then it stopped being a dream and became a – a target. A goal. I became obsessively interested in the astronauts who had died. And so I guess that's when it started.

I remember that so clearly, says Shaun. I remember watching it. That scared the shit out of me.

It scared the shit out of me too, Nell says.

They don't normally talk about these things. It makes a change from talking about station procedures, or rotas, or pinpointing and repairing docking leaks, or cleaning the bacteria filter, or replacing the inlet fan or heat exchanger. Or otherwise talking about TV shows they watched as kids, or books they loved; it turns out they were all familiar with Winnie-the-Pooh in one form or another in their five different countries. Winny-Puh l'orsetto, Pooh-san, Vinny Pukh: the same small animated bear there in some domain of their hearts. But when it comes to what got them here, what motives and desires, those things are behind them. They've got here, is what they think. You get here and your life starts anew and everything you brought along you brought in your head, and unless it's needed it stays in your head because this is it now. This is home.

Shaun makes himself coffee and Nell wonders whether to say what she's about to say. The crucifix he wears on a chain bobs up beneath his chin; this is why she always wants to ask him about his religion, because of that crucifix, so conspicuously present. He takes a packet of mixed nuts from his pocket, opens it, tosses a hazelnut into the air and approaches it open-mouthed like a trout.

Those seven astronauts who died on the *Challenger*, she says, I knew everything about their lives, everything.

Shaun sucks from the spout of the plastic coffee cup – comical, like supping from a toy watering can.

I was only seven, she says. I had pictures of them on my wall, the crew. I lit candles on their birthdays for, I don't know, three or so years after.

Shaun says, You did?

I did.

OK.

I wonder now that my father never tried to discourage this.

Shaun nods slowly in his appraising way, chewing, processing his image of this child lighting candles for dead astronauts; lighting candles full stop, dear God. But for astronauts. And yet why not; he used to set fibre-optic traps around his room to stop his sister trespassing. All children have their ways.

I was horrified, Nell says. I was horrified that they were there and then they were gone, in seventy seconds. Gone.

I mean, sure, Shaun says.

In seventy seconds, gone.

With the world watching, he says. Children watching.

Everybody watching, everybody—. Nell falters as if she's arrived at a precipice. When I was a child that thought stopped me sleeping, she says. The thought of how quickly everything can turn around. And my father, he just let me get on with it. Candles keep demons away, is what he once said, in a bid to comfort me – that's why you light them when you remember someone, to keep the demons from them. My father rarely said absurd things, but that was absurd. What use was protection from demons when you'd been in a space shuttle that had broken into five thousand pieces, when your compartment had fallen twelve miles at hundreds of miles an hour and smashed apart in the ocean? If there'd been demons, hadn't they already acted?

She remembers this clearly; finding some birthday candles and holders in the kitchen cupboard and planting them in plasticine and not daring for hours to strike a match, knowing she wasn't allowed them, thinking they might do something dangerous, explode in her hands perhaps.

Shaun doesn't answer, though there's nothing dismissive in that. He seems to be thinking. She too. Thinking of how she cried when the wreckage and the astronauts' bodies were recovered from the seabed over a month later, and how, in that grief which she couldn't even begin to understand, she buried herself in an obsession. Her father thinks she might still be burying herself in it now.

For a split second Shaun thinks, what the hell am I doing here, in a tin can in a vacuum? A tinned man in a tin can. Four inches of titanium away from death. Not just death, obliterated non-existence.

Why would you do this? Trying to live where you can never thrive? Trying to go where the universe doesn't want you when there's a perfectly good earth just there that does. He's never sure if man's lust for space is curiosity or ingratitude. If this weird hot longing makes him a hero or an idiot. Undoubtedly something just short of either.

The thoughts run into a wall and expire. Then are re-born into a sudden apprehension, for the hundredth time today, of those four souls, his colleagues and friends, on their way to the moon.

Take heart, his wife once said, if you perish up there the millions of bits of you will be orbiting the earth; that's a good thought isn't it? And smiled conspiratorially. And touched his earlobe in the way she does.

Ahoy mice, Chie whispers. Ahoy.

She takes the unit from the experiment rack and slides out a module, and the mouse inside cowers and tries to retreat. She scoops it up in her fingers. Around her the station radio burbles like a rain-swollen stream, burbles with moon talk now that it's afternoon and America has woken. *The first female astronaut to go to the moon, the great new leap for man- and womankind.*

There are five units of eight mice – those untouched by the hand of science (save for the rocket that propelled them here); those regularly injected to stop their muscles wasting, and those born modified, bulky and fit for a life without gravity.

Those untouched mice in groups one to three seem daily to be wasting away. In the one week since they arrived on the supply vehicle it's as though their souls have collapsed. Their black eyes bulge in shrinking bodies; their feet are large and useless, giving them the look of something aberrant and unevolved.

The mice in group four injected with the decoy receptor are bigger and sturdier. One by one Chie lifts them out and her thumb presses firmly on the back of the neck, and this way they know not to struggle, only to freeze; they fix their eyes on something that can't be guessed at. Even their felten folded batlike ears don't move. Her other thumb depresses the syringe gently. With release each mouse flows out of her hand and back to its cage.

The modified mice in group five, however, are bolder, as if they know by some instinct that their inflated size gives them greater advantage and power. When she reaches in to replace their food bars they come forward and squeal and take an interest in her hand, which is not so much bigger than they are. Whereas the untreated mice, whose muscles atrophy, fit like plums in her palm. She puts her mouth to their ears. I'm sorry, she whispers, but none of you get out of this alive. Not you small ones, not the big ones. You're all toast. I'm sorry to tell you.

The mice seem to take this news with a degree of stoicism. That's what you must be, she says. Always stoic. She strokes her thumb along a sharp spine. She will miss her mother's bone-picking ceremony, when they comb the ashes for fragments of bone that survived cremation. Missing that will be the hardest thing. The bone she'd most like to have found is the one that runs down the inside of the forearm, the ulna or radius, that long expressive bone she'd always see inside her mother's wrist while her mother was washing or brushing Chie's hair, the way its mechanism flexed and moved like a pulley. It had seemed so robotically perfect to Chie's young brain. That bone, or some little chipped part of it. Perhaps she'll ask her uncle to look.

In the galley Pietro eats his lunch of macaroni cheese. Well, they call it macaroni and they call it cheese. Before he left earth his teenage daughter had asked him: do you think progress is beautiful? Yes, yes, he'd said, not having to think. So beautiful, my God. But what about the atom bomb and what is it, these fake stars they're going to put into space in the shape of company logos, and the buildings they're going to print on the moon, out of its surface dust? Do we want buildings on the moon? she said. I love the moon as it is, she said. Yes, yes, he'd answered, me too, but all those things are beautiful, because their beauty doesn't come from their goodness, you didn't ask if progress is good, and a person is not beautiful because they're good, they're beautiful because they're alive, like a child. Alive and curious and restless. Never mind good. They're beautiful because there's a light in their eyes. Sometimes destructive, sometimes hurtful, sometimes selfish, but beautiful because alive. And progress is like that, by its nature alive.

All well and fine, but he hadn't been thinking then of the space-specification ready-to-eat macaroni cheese, which is neither good nor beautiful, nor made of anything that could ever possibly have had the will to live. He once tried to jazz it up with a bulb of fresh garlic that had come in the resupply vehicle. He heated some garlic cloves mixed with oil, in an old drinks sachet, thinking it would make an oily paste which he could drop into everything. But the sachet overheated and spilled and the oven, the galley, their sleeping quarters, the labs, smelled pungently of it for days, in fact weeks. In fact (since where do smells go in a sealed craft of infinitely recycled air) probably still does.

He can just about hear the radio. Something about Orion, brother of *Artemis*, the lunar astronauts' space-craft for their three-day journey and moon landing. Artemis, the goddess of the moon, the arrow-pouring goddess of the hunt. Strange how the most cutting-edge science brands itself with the gods and goddesses of myth. But regardless, which of them here would not want to be one of those astronauts on that crazed-god spacecraft? To stand on another body of rock that isn't the earth; is it necessarily the case that the further you get from something the more perspective you have on it? It's probably a childish thought, but he has an idea that if you could get far enough away from the earth you'd be able finally to understand it – to see it with your own eyes as an object, a small blue dot, a cosmic and mysterious thing. Not to understand its mystery, but to understand that it is mysterious. To see it as a math-ematical swarm. To see the solidity fall away from it.

In his lunch break Roman is trying to get the packet radio to work, but they're over the empty central reaches of Australia where nobody is, least of all a man or woman with ham radio. To his surprise some crackle comes but nothing distinct. Hello? he says. *Zdraste?* Velcroed to the wall in the Russian galley they have a photograph of Sergei Krikalev, the first Russian on the first expedition to the space station, the man who helped build it, the man who, before that, was sent to space by the USSR and was in orbit on *Mir* for almost six months longer than planned, because, while he was there, the USSR ceased to exist and he couldn't get home. Every day for a year he talked with a Cuban woman by packet radio who sent him news of his collapsing country. Roman's hero, Krikalev. His idol. An uncelebrated but quiet and clever and gentle man.

But you can't have it all, Pietro thinks, wiping his fork clean. There's not much seasoning in orbit and there's a lack of fresh bread, and the garlic experiment backfired, and your sense of taste and smell are in any case bombed out, but there's a euphoria that finds you with a velvet stealth, finds you in the blandest of moments, and you can feel the southern hemisphere stars through the craft's metal shell. Without even looking you can feel them copious and clustered. And his daughter is right to ask about progress, and he wishes he had not closed off the question with such certainty and sophistry since it's a question that comes from an innocence of mind and begs for the same in its answer. He should have said, I don't know my love. That would have been true. Because who can look at man's neurotic assault on the planet and find it beautiful? Man's hubris. A hubris so almighty it's matched only by his stupidity. And these phallic ships thrust into space are surely the most hubristic of them all, the totems of a species gone mad with self-love.

But what he meant to say to his daughter – and what he will say when he returns – is that progress is not a thing but a feeling, it's a feeling of adventure and expansion that starts in the belly and works up to the chest (and so often ends in the head where it tends to go wrong). It's a feeling he has almost perpetually when here, in both the biggest and smallest of moments – this belly-chest knowing of the deep beauty of things, and of some improbable grace that has shot him up here in the thick of the stars. A beauty he feels while he vacuums the control panels and air vents, as they eat their lunch separately and then dinner together, as they pile their waste into a cargo module to be launched towards earth where it'll burn up in the atmosphere and be gone, as the spectrometer surveys the planet, as the day becomes night which quickly becomes day, as the stars appear and disappear, as the continents pass beneath in infinite colour, as he catches a glob of toothpaste midair on his brush, as he combs his hair and climbs tired at the end of each day into his untethered sleeping bag and hangs neither upside down nor the right way up, because there is no right way up, a fact the brain comes to accept without argument, as he prepares to sleep two hundred and fifty miles above any ground for their falsely imposed night while outside the sun rises and sets fitfully. This is what Pietro wishes he could describe to his daughter, or, better, share with her (how he'd love her to come up here with him) – this soft, open witnessing of all that is well, that has presided with him for both of his missions. So maybe his answer was too certain, but how else could it have been when here, of all places in man's short but striving remit, is not somewhere to deny the beauty of progress?

I'll cut you a deal, Chie says to the mice. I'll come back and see you this evening if you get on with learning to fly. You can't keep clinging to the bars of the cage for the rest of the time you have, which isn't long I must tell you. You're going to crash into the Atlantic Ocean in a couple of months, and if you survive that you'll then be analysed in a lab and swiftly sacrificed to science. Got to let go, might as well do it now. You'll like it without gravity, you'll stop being afraid. Life is short (yours especially). Let go, be bold.

There they are, at the edge of Anton's view through the portal in the lab, the stars. The constellation of Centauri and the Southern Cross, Sirius and Canopus. The inverted Summer Triangle of Altair, Deneb and Vega. Anton tends to his wheat, which grows with a vigour that he sometimes finds touching, sometimes thrilling, sometimes sad, but he's stopped by a staggering blackness. Not the theatrical splendour of a hanging, spinning planet, but the booming silence of everything else, the *God knows what*. That's what Michael Collins called it as he orbited the dark side of the moon alone – Aldrin, Armstrong, earth and mankind all over there, and over here himself, and God knows what.

Shaun makes contact, via ground crews, with his astronaut friends on their way to the moon. They exchange understatements, as astronauts do. *A little bumpy on the way up but now she's sailing clean. Sure is a pretty sight out there.* He says he wishes he were going too, and this is true and false. He wishes it more than anything and he also misses his wife and won't abide the thought of going further from where she is. The moon is gibbous and gorgeously fat. Low to the atmosphere, its bottom half compressed out of shape like a sat-on cushion. There's pale light as they ascend north over the snow-capped cloud-flanked Andes, then the cloud thins and below is the Amazon, blistered and raw with fire.

Hello? says Roman into his packet radio to the disappearing continent of Australasia. *Zdraste?*

And a voice struggles back through the static and scratch. Are you there? Are you there, hello?

Orbit 5, descending

The earth is a place of circular systems: growth and decomposition, rainfall and evaporation, alive with the cycling of air currents that shunt the weather around the continents.

You know this of course, but in space you see it. The looping weather. This is what Nell could watch all day. A research meteorologist before she became an astronaut, she has an eye for the weather. How the earth drags at the air. See how the clouds at the equator are dragged up and eastward by the earth's rotation. All the moist warm air evaporating off the equatorial oceans and pulled in an arc to the poles, cooling, sinking, tugged back down in a westward curve. Ceaseless movement. Although, these words – drag, pull, tug – they describe the force of this movement but not its grace, not its – what? Its synchronicity/fluidity/harmony. None of those is quite the word. It's not so much that the earth is one thing and the weather another, but that they're the same. The earth is its air currents, the air currents the earth, just as a face is not separate from the expressions it makes.

What expression is this then, that she can see now? This typhoon that's another ninety minutes bigger, ninety minutes bolder, and closer to land. It's not anger, as people tend to say. It doesn't look from here anything like anger. More like defiance, strength, vivacity, the bulge-eyed tongue-out warrior face worn in the *haka*.

She photographs the typhoon's approach. It's extraordinary how she can see the curving of air that forms the trade winds, their sluicing westwards along the equator, churning up warmth from the surface of the ocean. The resulting banks of cloud form in columns drawing fuel from the ocean; the warmer the ocean, the larger the storm. She knows all this but she's never seen it so animate.

It's really something, this typhoon, Pietro says when he comes to join her. They watch it hone in on the Philippines and Taiwan and the coast of Vietnam. Its spiral flings clouds for hundreds of miles around a hole-punched siphoning eye.

They seem scarily frail, don't they, the Philippines, Pietro says. Little scraps of land that are first in line. They look like they could just wash away.

Nell nods. I've been diving there several times, she says.

I went to the Philippines on my honeymoon, he tells her. I went deep-sea diving in the Tubbataha reef, I've never seen a more incredible sight in my life, shapes and colours and creatures I could never have imagined. And I dived too off the island of Samar, I made friends with a fisherman, my wife and I had dinner with his family.

The people are amazing, Nell says, so warm and open. I went diving at Coron Bay among the wrecks, and at Barracuda Lake, and Malapascua – we went out at dawn one day and saw manta rays and thresher sharks, the sharks are like sickles, like polished steel, they look almost man-made except for their worried little faces, and they move like – like they're not moving, the water is undisturbed by them. I didn't see that but I saw a whale shark, says Pietro – did you see one? No, but I saw something I really wanted to see, a frogfish. Me too, says Pietro, my God, it was crazy, it was fantastic, bright yellow. And the sardine cloud, he says. Yes, Nell says, like a sea monster gliding past you. Just the light, Pietro says, streaming through the water. Just the depth of the colour blue, Nell agrees. Just the light, the colour, the creatures, the coral, the sounds, just everything. Pietro agrees: just everything.

Surprising things:
  The imagination
  Jackie Onassis's mode of death (lump in groin)
  The dinosaurs
  A blue pen with a red lid
  Green clouds
  Children in bow ties

When Chie heard of her mother's death she instantly went to one of the few earthly possessions she has in orbit – a photograph her mother gave her before she left to come here. In the photograph her mother is standing on the beach near their family home. She's in her youth. Aged twenty-four, before she had Chie, when she moved, freshly married, to the house by the sea. Her mother is on the beach in a thick woollen coat, though it was July and must have been hot. On the back of the photograph it says *Moon Landing Day, 1969* in her father's hand. Her mother is scowling up at the sky where a gull flies by at what seems like speed. The gull is blurred while her mother is sharp, still, narrow and small. It isn't clear whether her scowl is for the bird or the sky itself where she thinks the *Apollo* spaceship could be.

  For Chie, as a child, the photograph had a power she neither understood nor questioned. The lure of the absent

moon, the absent landing, the great proclaimed day that
was happening, but happening elsewhere. Mythical in
its remove. *Moon Landing Day*. She'd thought as a child
that it must have been what her mother was looking at
from the beach, something happening up on the moon,
and that her mother could see it with her naked eye. Or
as if her mother had been part of the event in some way.
And it wasn't until her mother gave her the photo before
this mission that she remembered those thoughts, and
felt their charge and the force of the past and how the
past is so stealthy in making the future – because she's
sure looking back that this photo had generated her first
thought of space.

On the photo's reverse now, under *Moon Landing Day,
1969*, it says, this time in her mother's hand, *For the next
and all moon landing days ever to come*. When Chie reads
it, it seems so unlike her mother to write such a thing
that she wonders if maybe her mother knew something,
a presaging of her own death, and thought to smuggle
in sentiment before she went. The thought leaves her
blank. She misses her mother. She misses her tough-
ness, her straightness, her distance. She expects that her
mother was one of a kind. How many others have lain in
a cot while an atomic bomb detonates? Not many. How
many others lost their mother to that bomb on a terrible

August day? Her mother's life was quiet and static, not
a bit like Chie's. Come to think of it, the photo of her
on the beach is a perfect emblem of that life, the world
blurring past her while she stayed still. But though their
lives couldn't be more different, all of Chie's courage
she owes to her mother. Her resilience and thickness of
skin and preparedness for anything, even the difficult
or painful or dangerous. Her daring and delight at the
difficult and dangerous. Her test-pilot brain that makes
her think flying and breathe flying and dream flying.
The sporting rivalry she has with death, which she's
winning and which makes her feel herself invincible,
unbruisable. Quietly, unexpectedly reckless.

She knows she is not – invincible that is. But she comes
from a line that slipped through the crack, the fissure
of history, found a way out while the whole thing came
down. Her grandfather unwell the day of the bomb and
sick from work and left with the baby, while her grandmother went to the market. There were no remains of
her grandmother. There were few remains of anyone
at the Nagasaki munitions factory where her grandfather worked and where he would have been if not unwell. Everybody in Japan was unwell by that time, after
years of war. Everybody was half-starved or had cholera
or dysentery or malaria or any old virus or infection

that rattled away in their bodies without hope of treat-ment – her grandfather had been unwell for a while with one of those viruses, and that was his first day off work. Why that day? If he'd been at work he would have died. If he'd not stayed at home the baby would not have stayed home with him; if the baby – Chie's mother – had gone to the market that day, her brief life would have met its end and Chie would not have later existed. Their family shuffled sideways through the crack of fate.

Chie looks hard at the photograph. They had it dis-played on one of the walls at home; she remembers her mother pointing it out. Look, Chie-chan, that's me the day the men went to the moon. Even now she doesn't know what she sees in that *Moon Landing Day* on the beach; she doesn't know what to read into the strange-ness of the scene, the incongruity of image and title. She examines her mother's face, interrogates the scowl for a clue as to what it denotes, but she doesn't know. Everything she reads into it is after the fact, superim-posed, and a guess at the truth. Why did the photograph end up on the wall when Chie was a child? What was so particular or telling or meaningful about it? Was it a mother saying to her daughter: and now I will show you what's possible in your life, the near-limitlessness of what humans, and therefore you, can do? But then why

the scowl, why not an expression of possibility or hope?
Or was she saying: here are some men reaching the
moon – do you see or hear a single woman among them,
much less a non-white, non-American woman, do you
notice that this is a collection of men in the full prime
of their masculinity with their rockets and thrusters
and payloads and the eyes of the world on them – this
is what the world is, a playground for men, a laboratory
for men, don't compete because any attempts at com-
petition will end in your feeling dispirited and inferior
and crushed, why run a race you can never win, why
set yourself up to fail – so please know, my daughter,
that you are not inferior and hold that grandly in your
heart and live your inconsequential life as well as you
can with a dignity of being, will you do that for me?

Or was she saying: look at these men going to the
moon, be afraid my child at what humans can do, because we know don't we what it all means, we know the
fanfare and glory of the pioneering human spirit and we
know the wonder of splitting the atom and we know
what these advances can do, your grandmother knew
it only too well when she stepped off the pavement to a
sound she didn't recognise and a flash that seemed both
distant and so close it might have happened inside her
own head, and in her bewilderment came a kernel of

knowledge that this might be it, a knowledge that gave rise instantly to a vision of me, her first and only child, which was the last vision she ever experienced, so I am saying to you Chie, my first and only child, that you might regard in wonder these men walking on the moon but you must never forget the price humanity pays for its moments of glory, because humanity doesn't know when to stop, it doesn't know when to call it a day, so be wary is what I mean though I say nothing, be wary.

For all the world it looks to Chie that she took the first of those possible messages and she took it as far as it could go even though it was the most ill-formed, the least credible, and she took it even though it might not have been what her mother meant, she took it and now here she is. She took her mother to mean: look at those men landing on the moon, look at what's possible given desire and belief and opportunity, and you have all of those if you want them, if they can do it you can do it, and by *it* I mean anything. Anything. Don't squander a life so miraculously given, since I, your mother, could just as easily have been with my mother that day at the market if any number of tiny things had been different, and I would have been among the youngest of the victims of the atomic bomb and circumstance could have killed me and you would never have been born. But you were born, and here we are, and here are these men on the moon, so you see, you are on the winning side, you are winning, and perhaps you can live a life that honours and furthers that? And Chie had said silently to her mother's silent request: yes, I see.

To herself, in her quarters, she gives a dumb nod, though she's not sure she does see; when it comes to it she doesn't know her mother at all. It's just imaginings and projections, and they could all be wrong.

Orbit 6

RUSSIAN COSMONAUTS ONLY, it says on the door of the Russian WC.

Correspondingly on the US toilet door, AMERICAN, EUROPEAN AND JAPANESE ATRONAUTS ONLY. *Because of ongoing political disputes please use your own national toilet.*

The idea of a national toilet has caused some amusement among the crew. I'm just going to take a national pee, Shaun will say. Or Roman: Guys, I'm going to go and do one for Russia.

You will have to now pay us to use our toilet facilities, the Russian Space Agency has said to those of America, Europe and Japan, and so those agencies have responded in kind: go right ahead, our toilet is in any case better than yours. And neither can you use our exercise bike. Well you can't access our food stores then. It's been like this now for over a year.

On the craft's internal cameras mission control watches the crew in flagrant disregard of these edicts

and there's no point trying to make it different. Astronauts and cosmonauts are much like cats, they conclude.
Intrepid, cool, and can't be herded.

We have all been travelling, the crew thinks, travelling for years with barely a moment of settling; all of
us living out of bags and borrowed places, hotels, space
centres and training facilities, sleeping on friends' sofas
in midway cities between one training course and another. Living in caves and submarines and deserts to test
our mettle. If we have any single thing in common it's
our acceptance of belonging nowhere and everywhere
in order to reach this, this near-mythical craft. This last
nationless, borderless outpost that strains against the
tethers of biological life. What does a toilet have to do
with anything? What use are diplomatic games on a
spacecraft, locked into its orbit of tender indifference?

And us? We are one. For now at least, we are one.
Everything we have up here is only what we reuse and
share. We can't be divided, this is the truth. We won't
be because we can't be. We drink each other's recycled
urine. We breathe each other's recycled air.

In the lab they drift with a virtual-reality headset and
an instructive voice asks warmly: count the number of
seconds a blue square appears in your vision. They guess

at eight seconds. Record this on the laptop. Thirty-six seconds. Twenty seconds. Three seconds. Twenty-nine seconds. Thank you, says the voice, and seems really to mean it. That was great, it says. Are you ready for the next task? Just hit Go when you are.

Now they must hold the blue square in their sight for different time durations which are given to them: five seconds, nineteen, four, thirty-eight. Then reaction times; how quickly do they touch a button on the laptop screen when the blue square appears. You did great, the voice says. Are you ready for the next task? Just hit Go when you are. For the first time this day America comes into sight portside in a polished mid-morning and soon rolls away.

Count to one minute and touch the screen when done.

Count to ninety seconds and touch the screen when done.

The minute, then the ninety seconds, seem to lose themselves midway, they're counting too fast they think, then change their minds, no, too slow; they skip ahead from forty-two to forty-five, and instantly regret it, and linger at fifty. That was great, the voice says.

While they look at blue squares the equator is crossed and there's a change of guard; the northern hemisphere comes and the moon has upturned. Its waxing light

which was on its left hand limb is now on its right. A
crêpe flipped in the pan. A thinning of stars. No longer the dense astral field of southern skies which look
toward the Milky Way's centre; now the stars they can
see are those far-flung, on the Milky Way's outer spi-
rals where the galaxy fades in amassing light years and
something gives way to less which gives way to nothing.
Then night-time cedes to another day. Over Venezuela
is that first blinding spike of light on the horizon that
they know well to be the sun. It spikes and goes, spikes
and goes. And then the right side of the earth's curve
becomes a gleaming scimitar. Silver pours out and the
stars are banished and the dark ocean turns to an instant dawn.

You did great, the voice says. You were wrong every
time! Too bad for you that when the blue square's there
for fifteen seconds you report ten; that your counted
minute is an extendable thing – a minute and a half
or sometimes more. Too bad for you, it consoles, that
you've drifted too long, you've floated too long, that the
clocks in your cells have gone off their pace. Too bad for
you that when you wake up in the morning you don't
know where your arm is until you look, that without
the feedback of weight your limbs are mislaid. (Where
did I put it, that arm? says the panicked brain. Where

did I leave it?) Too bad for you that your limbs are lost
in space and that those lost in space are lost too in time.
That you're losing your grip. That when you snatch
lightning-fast at a pair of pliers sailing by, your split
second is a lumbering two or three, that time around
you is growing idle and plump. That you are no longer
the sharp tool you used to be. Too bad for you that the
Omega Speedmaster watch on your wrist with its chro-
nograph and tachymeter and coaxial escapement has no
grasp of the fact that this is your seventh time around
the earth since you woke up this morning, that the sun
is up-down-up-down like a mechanical toy. Too bad
for you that your world's gone elastic and topsy-turvy
and right-side-left and that now it's spring and in half
an hour it's autumn and your body clock's blitzed and
your senses have slowed and your superfast astronaut
uber-being self has gone a bit loose and carefree and
swimmy like seaweed or jetsam. Are you ready for the
next task? Just hit Go when you are.

The seconds dissolve and mean less and less. Time
shrinks to a dot on a field of blank white, specific and
senseless, then bloats without edges and loses its shape.
They pounce on the cursor whenever they're asked,
quick as a flash, not quick at all. Europe moves below in
an afternoon haze and the clouds mark out the shape of

coastlines. There's the south-west toe of England kicking limply at the North Atlantic, there's the English Channel, blink and you've missed it, there's Brussels and Amsterdam and Hamburg and Berlin, though they're drawn in invisible ink on grey-green felt, there's Denmark in its dolphin-leap towards Norway and Sweden, there's the Baltic Sea and the Baltic States and suddenly Russia. Here came Europe, there went Europe. What a shame, says the voice still warmly, that you exist in all time zones and none at all, that you shift across longitudes in this great metal albatross, that more is asked of your brain than it knows how to do. Too bad for you that it all goes so quickly. That a continent lapses and gives way to another, that the earth, so beloved, never stays in your grasp. That the ride of your life will pass in an eyeblink, just as life does to the aging brain whose slowing makes everything appear to move faster. Too bad for you that before you know it you'll be back in your landing capsule with its heat shield and parachute and you'll crash through the atmosphere engulfed in fire and down you'll go in a trail of plasma, and you'll land God willing on a plain vaster than vision and be pulled from the capsule with pipe-cleaner legs and spluttering monosyllables where once was language.

At the brink of a continent the light is fading. The sea is flat and copper with reflected sun and the shadows of the clouds are long on the water. Asia come and gone. Australia a dark featureless shape against this last breath of light, which has now turned platinum. Everything is dimming. The earth's horizon, which cracked open with light at so recent a dawn, is being erased. Darkness eats at the sharpness of its line as if the earth is dissolving and the planet turns purple and appears to blur, a watercolour washing away.

Orbit 7

The orbit hunts northwards. They're approaching Central America when the twilight zone that is the Terminator rushes beneath dragging morning behind. When the sun rises for the seventh time this day, swift and total, the light reaches them before it reaches earth and the craft is a burning bullet.

Somehow, Nell thinks, once you've been on a spacewalk, looking at space through a window is never the same. It's like looking through bars at an animal you once ran with. An animal that could have devoured you yet chose instead to let you into the flank-quivering pulse of its exotic wildness.

At first, on her spacewalk last week, she'd felt that she was falling. For a moment it was terrible. When the hatch is released, when you emerge into it from the airlock and struggle free, when you let go, there are two objects you can see in the universe – the space station and the earth. Don't look down, you're told – focus on your hands, on your task, until you've adjusted. She looked down, how could she not? The earth was tumbling beneath her at speed. The naked startling earth. From out there it doesn't have the appearance of a solid thing, its surface is fluid and lustrous. Then she looked at her hands, which were large and spectral white in their gloves, and she saw her fellow astronaut ahead of her, Pietro, gliding out against profound darkness, the spectrometer they planned to install floating beside him, and he was a bird released to an unimagined freedom.

You check your tethers; you navigate around the craft using the handrails; you must protect whatever equipment you take out there with you, the cargo of batteries clipped to your suit, the antenna or the unit or the replacement panel, you must not get tangled in the tethers, but it's hard to move inside the suits, hard to steer when the mass of the spacesuit is throwing your centre of gravity. You think of the training you did in water and how the still water of the training pool holds you in a way that space doesn't, how space has a ferocity and wants (though without malice, with nothing but empty indifference) to tilt you, upend and undo you, and you remember then not to fight it, only to adapt to it. More like surfing in that respect, and it's then that you look down with a fuller view, as if to check that the earth and its seas are not just dreams or mirages, and there it is again, earth, turning blue and cloud-scudded and improbably soft against the truss of the craft you are navigating around. No longer frightening at all, instead a sight of such magnificence it shoots your senses apart. Your tether swinging, your feet hanging, your suit chafing painfully at the elbows, clipping yourself to the reels as you climb the truss. Away to the left, a communications satellite spins in its orbit.

She was outside for hours – almost seven, so she was told. You have no idea at all of the passing of time. You install or repair whatever you are tasked to install or repair; you photograph some of the hatches, the external tools, you do a litter-pick of debris, plucking from space a few of these tens of thousands of remnants of jettisoned or exploded satellites and launch-vehicle stages and craft; wherever mankind goes it leaves some kind of destruction behind it, perhaps the nature of all life, to do this. Dusk steals upon you and the earth is a bruising of azure and purple and green, and you remove your sun visor and turn on your light and darkness brings out the stars and Asia passes by bejewelled and you work in your light-pool until the sun comes up once more behind you and burnishes an ocean you can't identify. Daylight spills blue on a snowy landmass moving into view and, against the black, the rim of the earth is a light bright mauve that brings a pain of elation to the gut. What might be the Gobi Desert rolls out beneath you while ground crews give soothing instructions and your partner leafs through the manual attached to the arm of his spacesuit and you can just about see his face through the sun visor, a tranquil oval of a human face in the enormous anonymity of your landscape, and meanwhile the solar arrays drink the sun until dusk comes back and your partner is blackened by the sunset behind him and night creeps from the under- side of the earth and engulfs it.

Nell had dreams of flying when she was a child and then later a teenager. The others did too, each one of them. Short dreams of surging flight or long and languid dreams of discovery, in any case dreams of breaking or being free. The flying they did, or still do, in dreams is the closest analogy they have to moving in space, these dreams share the same weightless ease and the same sense of miracle, because it ought to be impossi- ble for a heavy wingless body to be gliding this freely and smoothly and yet here it is and it seems that you are finally doing the thing for which your being was born. It is hard to believe. At the same time, it is hard to

believe in anything else. It is hard to believe the qual-
ity of blackness that is the entirety of space around a
day-lit earth, where the earth absorbs all the light – yet
hard to believe in anything but that blackness, which
is alive, and breathing and beckoning. If Nell had ever
been afraid of nothingness, once she was in it she was
consoled by it inexplicably and yearned – if she yearned
for anything out there – to drift into it and for her tether
to reel out some thousands of miles.

You look down the length of your own body hanging
to the rig while you grapple with the pistol-grip tool
and the torque multiplier and the old bolts that have
got stuck and which you have no force of gravity to
remove, and two hundred and fifty miles beneath your
feet the buffed orb of earth hangs too like an hallucina-
tion, something made by and of light, something you
could pass through the centre of, and the only word that
seems to apply to it is *unearthly*. It can't possibly be real.
Forget all you know. You look back at the vast spread of
the space station and in this moment it, not earth, feels
like home. Inside the craft the four others. But out there,
forget all you know. Her heart and Pietro's the only ones
to beat in space between the earth's atmosphere and as
far out beyond the solar system as anyone can guess.

Their two heartbeats speeding peacefully through it, never in the same place twice. Never to return to the same place again.

When the six of them talked about their spacewalks afterwards, they described déjà vu – they *knew* they'd been there before. Roman said that perhaps it was caused by untapped memories of being in the womb. That's what being floating in space feels like for me, he'd said. Being not yet born.

Here is Cuba pink with morning.

The sun bounces everywhere off the ocean's surface. The turquoise shallows of the Caribbean and the horizon conjuring the Sargasso Sea.

To be out there, Nell thinks, to have no glass or metal between her and this. Just a spacesuit filled with coolant to ward off the sun's heat. Just a spacesuit and piece of rope and her slender life.

Just her feet dangling above a continent, her left foot obscuring France, her right foot Germany. Her gloved hand blotting out western China.

At first they're drawn to the views at night – the gorgeous encrusting of city lights and the surface dazzle of man-made things. There's something so crisp and clear and purposeful about the earth by night, its thick embroidered urban tapestries. Almost every mile of Europe's coastline is inhabited and the whole continent outlined with fine precision, the cities constellations joined by the golden thread of roads. Those same golden threads track across the Alps, usually greyish blue with snowfall.

At night they can point to home – there's Seattle, Osaka, London, Bologna, St Petersburg and Moscow – Moscow one enormous point of light like the Pole Star in a shrill clear sky. The night's electric excess takes their breath. The spread of life. The way the planet proclaims to the abyss: there is something and someone here. And how, for all that, a sense of friendliness and peace prevails, since even at night there's only one man-made border in the whole of the world; a long trail of lights between Pakistan and India. That's all civilisation has to show for its divisions, and by day even that has gone.

Soon things change. After a week or so of city awe, the senses begin to broaden and deepen and it's the daytime earth they come to love. It's the humanless simplicity of land and sea. The way the planet seems to breathe, an animal unto itself. It's the planet's indifferent turning in indifferent space and the perfection of the sphere which transcends all language. It's the black hole of the Pacific becoming a field of gold or French Polynesia dotted below, the islands like cell samples, the atolls opal lozenges; then the spindle of Central America which drops away beneath them now to bring to view the Bahamas and Florida and the arc of smoking volcanoes on the Caribbean Plate. It's Uzbekistan in an expanse of ochre and brown, the snowy mountainous beauty of Kyrgyzstan. The clean and brilliant Indian Ocean of blues untold. The apricot desert of Takla Makan traced about with the faint confluencing and parting lines of creek beds. It's the diagonal beating path of the galaxy, an invitation in the shunning void.

So then come discrepancies and gaps. They were warned in their training about the problem of dissonance. They were warned about what would happen with repeated exposure to this seamless earth. You will see, they were told, its fullness, its absence of borders except those between land and sea. You'll see no countries, just a rolling indivisible globe which knows no possibility of separation, let alone war. And you'll feel yourself pulled in two directions at once.

Exhilaration, anxiety, rapture, depression, tenderness, anger, hope, despair. Because of course you know that war abounds and that borders are something that people will kill and die for. While up here there might be the small and distant rucking of land that tells of a mountain range and there might be a vein that suggests a great river, but that's where it ends. There's no wall or barrier – no tribes, no war or corruption or particular cause for fear.

Before long, for all of them, a desire takes hold. It's the desire – no, the need (fuelled by fervour) – to protect this huge yet tiny earth. This thing of such miraculous and bizarre loveliness. This thing that is, given the poor choice of alternatives, so unmistakably home. An unbounded place, a suspended jewel so shockingly bright. Can humans not find peace with one another? With the earth? It's not a fond wish but a fretful demand. Can we not stop tyrannising and destroying and ransacking and squandering this one thing on which our lives depend? Yet they hear the news and they've lived their lives and their hope does not make them naive. So what do they do? What action to take? And what use are words? They're humans with a godly view and that's the blessing and also the curse.

It seems easier on balance not to read the news. Some
do and some don't, but it's easier not to. When they look
at the planet it's hard to see a place for or trace of the
small and babbling pantomime of politics on the news-
feed, and it's as though that pantomime is an insult to
the august stage on which it all happens, an assault on
its gentleness, or else too insignificant to be bothered
with. They might listen to the news and feel instantly
tired or impatient. The stories a litany of accusation,
angst, anger, slander, scandal that speaks a language
both too simple and too complex, a kind of talking in
tongues, when compared to the single clear, ringing
note that seems to emit from the hanging planet they
now see each morning when they open their eyes. The
earth shrugs it off with its every rotation. If they listen
to the radio at all it's often for music or else something
with an innocence or ultimate neutrality about it, com-
edy or sport, something with a sense of play, of things
mattering and then not mattering, of coming and going
and leaving no mark. And then even those they listen
to less and less.

But then one day something shifts. One day they look
at the earth and they see the truth. If only politics really
were a pantomime. If politics were just a farcical, inane,

at times insane entertainment provided by characters who for the most part have got where they are, not by being in any way revolutionary or percipient or wise in their views, but by being louder, bigger, more ostentatious, more unscrupulously wanting of the play of power than those around them, if that were the beginning and end of the story it would not be so bad. Instead, they come to see that it's not a pantomime, or it's not just that. It's a force so great that it has shaped every single thing on the surface of the earth that they had thought, from here, so human-proof.

Every swirling neon or red algal bloom in the polluted, warming, overfished Atlantic is crafted in large part by the hand of politics and human choices. Every retreating or retreated or disintegrating glacier, every granite shoulder of every mountain laid newly bare by snow that has never before melted, every scorched and blazing forest or bush, every shrinking ice sheet, every burning oil spill, the discolouration of a Mexican reservoir which signals the invasion of water hyacinths feeding on untreated sewage, a distorted flood-bulged river in Sudan or Pakistan or Bangladesh or North Dakota, or the prolonged pinking of evaporated lakes, or the Gran Chaco's brown seepage of cattle ranch where once was rainforest, the expanding green-blue geometries of evaporation ponds where lithium is mined from the brine, or Tunisian salt flats in *cloisonné* pink, or the altered contour of a coastline where sea is reclaimed metre by painstaking metre and turned into land to house more and more people, or the altered contour of a coastline where land is reclaimed metre by metre by a sea that doesn't care that there are more and more people in need of land, or a vanishing mangrove forest in Mumbai, or the hundreds of acres of greenhouses which make the entire southern tip of Spain reflective in the sun.

The hand of politics is so visible from their vantage point that they don't know how they could have missed it at first. It's utterly manifest in every detail of the view, just as the sculpting force of gravity has made a sphere of the planet and pushed and pulled the tides which shape the coasts, so has politics sculpted and shaped and left evidence of itself everywhere.

They come to see the politics of want. The politics of growing and getting, a billion extrapolations of the urge for more, that's what they begin to see when they look down. They don't even need to look down since they, too, are part of those extrapolations, they more than anyone –on their rocket whose boosters at lift-off burn the fuel of a million cars.

The planet is shaped by the sheer amazing force of human want, which has changed everything, the forests, the poles, the reservoirs, the glaciers, the rivers, the seas, the mountains, the coastlines, the skies, a planet contoured and landscaped by want.

Orbit 8, ascending

If you know where to look and you get a large zoom lens and close right in, you can see the man-made craters in the desert in Arizona that were dynamited out to resemble the moon. Here in the sixties Armstrong and Aldrin trained for their landing, though they're going now, those craters, eroding away.

New Mexico, Texas, Kansas, borderless states and invisible cities on the wide dry cowhide of the south-west American belt. The clouds are wind-warped and ribbony and travelling. Here and there a momentary flash which signals the sun reflecting off the hull of an aeroplane; the plane can't be seen, only the flash. And across this great leathery hide are nonsensical scorings, indentations pressed into a surface, which of course are rivers but which have no flow. They seem dry, static, accidental and abstract. They seem like strands of long fallen hair.

On the curve of the earth, fast approaching, is a mossier tinge, a land less arid; then a finger of blue with a depth of black. Lake Michigan, Lake Superior, Lake Huron, Lake Ontario, Lake Erie. Their centres beaten steel in the afternoon sun.

The past comes, the future, the past, the future. It's always now, it's never now.

It's 5 p.m. on their looping spacecraft. On the earth beneath them, where Toronto is just appearing, it's still midday. On the other side of the world it's already tomorrow and the other side of the world will arrive in forty minutes.

Over there, in tomorrow, the typhoon summons winds of a hundred and eighty miles per hour. It's rampaging through the Mariana Islands. The sea levels off the islands' coasts have already risen with the expansion of the warmer water, and now, where the winds push the sea toward the westward edges of its basin, the sea rises more and a five-metre storm surge engulfs the islands of Tinian and Saipan. It's as though the islands are hit with cluster bombs – windows blown out, walls buckling, furniture flying, trees splicing.

Nobody foresaw the rapid growth of this typhoon, which in twenty-four hours has gone from a seventy-mile-an-hour skirmish in the middle ocean to a charging force closing in on land. The meteorologists who see the images of it now raise its level to a Category Five and some think typhoon and some think super-typhoon and there's nothing to do but predict its landfall at the Philippines to the nearest hour. The hour, they say, will be 10 a.m. local time, 2 a.m. up here.

It's all in the future on the earth's other side, occurring on a day that hasn't yet arrived. The crew go on with the last of their tasks. Anton eats an energy bar to fight off late afternoon drowsiness. Shaun removes the four fasteners on the bracket of the smoke detector that needs replacing. Chie inspects the bacteria filters. Their path now ups and overs and exits America where the Atlantic is ancient, the placid silver-grey of a dug-up brooch. Calm suffuses this hemisphere. And with no ceremony they complete another lap of the lonely planet. They top out some three hundred miles off the Irish coast.

In passing through the lab, Nell looks out and sees the promise of Europe on the watery horizon. She feels somehow speechless. Speechless at the fact of her loved ones being down there on that stately and resplendent sphere, as if she's just discovered they've been living all along in the palace of a king or queen. People *live* there, she thinks. *I* live there. This seems improbable to her today.

⋆   ⋆   ⋆

Roman, Nell and Shaun arrived here three months ago, a trio of astronauts folded into a module the size of a two-man tent. They docked to the station and the capsule's probe penetrated neatly the spacecraft's drogue. Soft capture. A bee entering a flower. The spacecraft's eight mechanical hooks locked the module in. Hard capture, confirm, hard capture complete. A stilling inside the module and a moment's pause. Roman, Nell and Shaun had turned to one another and high-fived with sailing hands that hadn't figured out what it meant to be weightless. Roman had cupped lightly the felt moon his son had given him, that hung in front of them on the voyage, a mascot, now bobbing. In the grandness of space even that mascot had utmost dignity. Everything was capped with potential. They could barely speak.

Stillness more and stillness again and stillness blooming into the hearts of the crew. It had been six hours of exhilarating speed, and now nothing. Now in harbour. How could it be that six hours ago you were on terra firma? Unfold your legs, pull yourself from your seat into the orbital module and stretch your crooked back.

They were held for some two hours while they waited for the leak checks to be finished and for the pressure between the crafts to equalise. On the other side of the hatch was the awaiting crew who'd arrived three months before. Anton, Pietro, Chie. They knocked, clack-clack on the hatch, and a series of knocks came back. They'd come this far, and were only some eighteen inches from the inside of that spaceship that would be their home for several months, only eighteen inches from everything towards which they'd been aiming for so long. Yet had to wait and wait, in some antechamber which felt in a sense biblical, a pause between life and the afterlife. In some respects, for those two hours, you don't exist in any way you can recognise. Nothing you've ever experienced has been experienced that far from the surface of the earth and nothing you're about to experience is really yet known. And you're exhausted in a way you've never been before. And incredulous at microgravity, at your nasal voice which doesn't sound like yourself.

Diligently they waited for the mercury to show the pressure was equal – it must reach seven four six, seven four seven before opening the hatch. Roman's eyes were unable to lift from the pressure gauge. Then he attached the crank handle and turned it slowly and the crew on the other side pulled as he pushed and he heard their voices, *that's it, we're there, here it comes*, as the hatch opened with a great heaving weariness at odds with a nauseous wash of euphoria that engulfed him. Engulfed them all. A roll of uncertain laughter, and faces appeared, Pietro, my friend; Chie, dear Chie *moy drug*; Anton, my brother. Here's the module they had all known so long through flight simulations, their bodies delivered bumpily through the hatch, six of them suddenly in the same small space, a mass of amazed life. A flurry of handshakes and long embraces, of hellos and welcomes, of *my God*, of *can you believe this*, of *we made it, you made it, dobro pozalovat, welcome, welcome and welcome back*. Whistling. Anton brought bread and salt as per the Russian tradition of hospitality. Or in any case crackers and salt cubes. They all partook.

There were just moments of this and then before they knew it they found themselves with a headset and microphone and on a screen were their families, beaming. Except that it's not your family and it's not your living room you see in the background, but something you knew from another life that comes to you now with a vague recollection. They stumbled through some words that were erased from memory as soon as they were spoken but their brains were hijacked and tumbling and they couldn't see for tiredness and their limbs were askance. Even for Roman who'd been here twice before. It takes some adjustment. It gives your body a pummelling. There's the first dumbfounding view of earth, a hunk of tourmaline, no a cantaloupe, an eye, lilac orange almond mauve white magenta bruised textured shellac-ed splendour.

That night Roman's felt moon spun in front of him in delirious sleep. He saw images of his son in states of need or peril. A pain in his forehead blew like a hatchet, and he worried that the sound of his vomiting would keep others awake. In the US section Shaun was worrying the same.

In the morning everything, but everything, was new. Their clothes were creased from the packet, their toothbrush and towel in their cellophane. Their sports shoes crisp and roomy around their bloodless feet and the blood that was there travelling upwards to shape their faces in a relentless expression of sleepy surprise. The earth outside was made that day and was at the same time the oldest of things. Their minds were freshly minted. The sickness was gone, as if they'd been purged. Roman taught Nell and Shaun, who hadn't been here before, the art of moving. Your body can float, can fly; not human! You can swim albeit giddily through air. Just repeat the mantra as you go: slow is smooth and smooth is fast, slow is smooth and smooth is fast. And day by day the tethers of their lives have broken one after the other and everything they are now is a new invention. That's how it is, Pietro once told Roman, and he agreed, that's how it is.

Just a few weeks here leaves you paler and thinner. If humans were to stay long enough in space would they eventually take on the form of something amphibious, Pietro wonders. He's been here now almost six months and has three months more. He thinks he's becoming a tadpole, all head and no body. With the atrophying of the body life doesn't tug at him so much. He feels hungry so he eats, and the sinuses are so blocked that the food has no taste; but anyway there's no real appetite, not really. He sleeps because he must, but his sleep is mostly tentative, not deep or robust as it is on earth. Everything in his body seems to lack commitment to the cause of its animal life, as if there's a cooling of systems, an efficient running-down of superfluous parts. In the slowing and cooling he hears his thoughts more, they're distant bells chiming one at a time in his head. In orbit his sense of life is simpler and gentler and more forgiving, not that his thoughts are different but that his thoughts are fewer and more distinct. They don't avalanche like they used to. They come and they interest him for as long as they need to and then they go.

There were some nights, about a month in, that he thought of his wife with an insane and afflictive longing, he thought of her bony nudity, tan lines, dark underarm hair, rack of ribs, tied wrists, sweat on her breasts in the siesta heat. The thoughts left him momentarily embittered and drunk with longing. A week after that he did his spacewalk with Nell, and the next night she, Nell, appeared in a dream that involved some setting on earth he wasn't familiar with, a room in absolute darkness that seemed cramped and was, in his mind, panelled with wood, but in which Nell's voice came from far away although her body was up against his. It was so surprising to find her there that something ecstatic had gone through his core. There was a party happening out of sight – he could just hear the music but had no real sense of where it was. He held her up against him and kissed her neck and repeated her name in awe. That's all he remembers and the next day at breakfast he could barely look at her, so embarrassed he was.

The dream hasn't repeated, and it felt then that any last note of sexuality in his body quietened. It seemed to understand there was no point, and a switch was flicked off, and all went blank and calm.

Orbit 8, descending

When Nell went freediving she would think: maybe this is how it is to be an astronaut. Now up here she sometimes closes her eyes and thinks: this is like diving. The slow suspended way the body moves, calmly carried as if in water. And the way they move around the labyrinth of the spaceship as if around a wreck – the constricted spaces, the hatches that open into narrow tubes that warren this way and that in near-identical patterns, until it's hard to know where you started from or where the earth will be when you look out. And when you do look out any claustrophobia becomes agoraphobia in an instant, or you have both at once.

She hauls cargo bags from one place to another. Everything burnable, everything not to go back to earth, goes into stowage; bags of food waste, rubbish, used tissues and toilet paper and wipes, trousers, T-shirts, socks, underwear and towels, gym clothes steeped in weeks of sweat, old tubes of toothpaste, every sachet of every meal and drink they've had, nail and hair cuttings, all of it to go, eventually, into the resupply craft that arrives next week, so that when it undocks in two months the whole lot will combust in the atmosphere, and any debris left will begin its long life of earth orbit. The task becomes blindly physical, shunting large cargo cubes about in a 3D puzzle. It's like a caravan here; there's too little room, everything is crammed everywhere, you push it down with your feet and strap it fast before it can float away. When she passes Anton in a doorway they turn on their sides and glide front-to-front, her nose brushing the slight bulge of his belly.

There was a caravanning holiday she had which couldn't have been long before her mother died. Perhaps she was four or five. Just as she is now, her mother was shoving bags wherever they would go, in the small kitchen cupboards whose laminate was peeling off, in the trunks under the table seats, in the tiny bedroom wardrobe, in the overhead cupboards whose magnetic catches clicked (the sound all day long was click-click-click), her mother quietly industrious as if they were moving in, not on holiday. And they did move around often, and there was a time 'between homes' as her father later said (where? she always imagined at some distant relative's or a friend's), but he didn't mention a caravan and if they'd lived in one, for however long, she'd have surely remembered.

A low light outside – the late afternoon sobriety of what she knows instantly to be northern Europe, complex with cloud, under which there are numberless shades of brown. The south coast of Ireland – where her husband is – and England portside; they skirt below these coasts before going south through the centre of Europe. There's such steady purpose to the way they orbit, the way they seem always to climb toward the pale crest of the earth, never to reach it. But going with such patience and purpose nevertheless. And as they traverse south the colours change, the browns lighter, the palette less sombre, a range of greens from the dark of the mountainsides to the emerald of river plains to the teal of the sea. The rich purplish-green of the vast Nile Delta. Brown becomes peach becomes plum; Africa beneath them in its abstract batik. The Nile is a spillage of royal-blue ink.

Her husband says that Africa from space looks like a late Turner; those near-formless landscapes of thick impasto shot with light. He'd told her once that if he were ever to be where she is, he'd spend his whole time in tears, helpless in the face of the earth's bare beauty. But that he'd never be where she is because he's a man who disappoints himself with his need of firm ground. He needs stability inside and out, and to simplify his life lest it overwhelm him. There are people like him (so he says) who complicate their inner lives by feeling too much all at once, by living in knots, and who therefore need outer things to be simple. A house, a field, some sheep for example. And there are those who manage somehow, by some miracle of being, to simplify their inner lives so that outer things can be ambitious and limitless. Those people can swap out a house for a spaceship, a field for a universe. And though he'd give his leg to be the latter, it's not the kind of thing you can trade a leg for – in any case who'd want his leg if they already had limitlessness?

Nobody has limitlessness, she'd said. He asked her then if she'd ever go to Mars, knowing the journey would be at least three years and that she might never come back. Yes, she'd answered without a moment's hesitation, and it was hard for her to understand why anyone would choose otherwise. I *want* to want to, he'd said. I want to be the kind of person who wants to go to Mars, but I'd go mad on the way, I'd be the one who cracked up and threatened the mission, they'd have to euthanise me for the greater good. Come on, she'd said kindly (though in essence she thought he was probably right).

The last of the cargo bags to move today she puts in the airlock, with the spacesuits – ghostly floating things, touched with the rawness of space. Will she ever go back out in one of these? That really was like freediving, being outside of the craft. There was a time she went freediving at night through bioluminescence – stars sparking all around. Your lungs packed with air, your body and the water equalising and becoming continuous with one another, the mind tranquil and gathered.

She and her husband exchange photographs almost daily; sometimes his view of the lough and the mountain and a bloodied sunset, sometimes a close-up of an icicle or sheep ear or flower or gatepost, sometimes the sea or the clouds reflected in the wet sand, once the night sky and a drawn circle where their spacecraft was travelling across – not visible in the photo but a caption: *You Are Were Here*. By the time you get this, he wrote in his message, you'll have been round the world another eight or nine times. You've got to admit that it's difficult, he said, having a wife flying above you at seventeen thousand miles an hour. Never knowing where she is or where to find her.

In return she sends him pictures of the earth, of the stars and moon, of the sleeping quarters and crew mates and dinners and modules. Of Ireland, which is always at least partly under cloud. Of her on a bike in stark constantly stimulating fluorescent light, amid the clutter of cables, wires, experiment racks, cameras, computers, ducts, vents, bars, hatches, switches, panels. The truth is, he always knows where to find her. Her exact location is a publicly known and closely mapped fact, a set orbit predictable to the millisecond. She could be in any of the seventeen modules, but nowhere else. Except just that once outside in space – but even then watched by hundreds and closely tethered.

She is, it must be said, trapped. It's his whereabouts that are less known; he could be anywhere. Of the six years of their relationship they've been married for five; of those five years she's been in astronaut training for four; of those four years they've spent only a handful of months together, and not even a third of those have been spent in his family home in Ireland which he inherited and moved into last year with a suitcase of things, because if he was going to be largely alone then better there than their flat in London where he had no garden or space or sense of himself. So now he pursues a life in a country she barely knows, a land as mythical to her as these earth views are to him. A land of reeds and bog cotton and gorse and fuchsia. His land, a photo of him in his fields in a sunset that blazed him to a silhouette, an absence. (A photo taken by whom?)

So she asked him, Who is the more unknown? And his reply to that: Both differently but equally unknown. Your mind full of acronyms and mine full of sheep ailments. Both of us equally unknown.

Orbit 9

Hello? says Roman into the radio. *Zdraste?* Hello?
Hello?
Zdraste, hello.
Is that really you? Is that space? Are you an astronaut?
A cosmonaut, *zdraste*, hello.
Pardon?
How are you?
I'm Tony.
I'm Roman.
I said Tony.
I know.
I can't hear you.
I'm Roman.
It's crackly and kind of faint.
I'm Roman, a cosmonaut.
How are you?
I'm well, how are you?
I'm Tony.

★   ★   ★

Pressing past the heliosphere in interstellar space are the two contraptions known as *Voyager 1* and *Voyager 2*, great coffee grinders wimbling into wayless dark. High-gain antenna, low-field magnetometer, high-field magnetometer, hydrazine thrusters, cosmic ray, yawing, pitching thirteen billion miles from earth and toward eternity. And on each one's bus which houses the electronics is mounted a golden disc that could be a plaque or a portal but is in fact a phonograph, a vinyl, filled with sounds of earth.

One day in the next five hundred billion years, while the probes complete one full circuit of the Milky Way, maybe they'll stumble upon intelligent life. In forty thousand years or so, when the two probes sail close enough to a planetary system, maybe just maybe one of these planets will be home to some life form which will spy the probe with whatever it has that passes for eyes, stay its telescope, retrieve the derelict fuel-less old probe with whatever it has that passes for curiosity, lower the stylus (supplied) to the record with whatever it has that passes for digits, and set free the dadada-daa of Beethoven's Fifth. It'll roll like thunder through a different frontier. Human music will permeate the Milky

Way's outer reaches. There'll be Chuck Berry and Bach, there'll be Stravinsky and Blind Willie Johnson, and the didgeridoo, violin, slide guitar and shakuhachi. Whale song will drift through the constellation of Ursa Minor. Perhaps a being on a planet of the star AC+793888 will hear the 1970s recording of sheep bleat, laughter, footsteps and the soft pluck of a kiss. Perhaps they'll hear the trundle of a tractor and the voice of a child.

When they hear on the phonograph a recording of rapid firecracker drills and bursts, will they know that these sounds denote brainwaves? Will they ever infer that over forty thousand years before in a solar system unknown a woman was rigged to an EEG and her thoughts recorded? Could they know to work backwards from the abstract sounds and translate them once more into brainwaves, and could they know from these brainwaves the kinds of thoughts the woman was having? Could they see into a human's mind? Could they know she was a young woman in love? Could they tell from this dip and rise in the EEG's pattern that she was thinking simultaneously of earth and lover as if the two were continuous? Could they see that, though she tried to keep to her mental script, to bring to mind Lincoln and the Ice Age and the hieroglyphs of ancient Egypt

and whatever grand things had shaped the earth and
which she wished to convey to an alien audience, every
thought cascaded into the dark brows and proud nose
of her lover, the wonderful articulation of his hands and
the way he listened like a bird and how they had touched
so often without touching. And then a spike in sound as
she thought of that great city Alexandria and of nuclear
disarmament and the symphony of the earth's tides and
the squareness of his jaw and the way he spoke with such
bright precision so that everything he said was epiphany
and discovery and the way he looked at her as though
she were the epiphany he kept on having and the thud
of her heart and the flooding of heat about her body
when she considered what it was he wanted to do to
her and the migration of bison across a Utah plain and a
geisha's expressionless face and the knowledge of having
found that thing in the world which she ought never
to have had the good fortune of finding, of two minds
and bodies flung at each other at full dumbfounding
force so that her life had skittered sidelong and all her
pin-boned plans just gone like that and her self engulfed
in a fire of longing and thoughts of sex and destiny, the
completeness of love, their astounding earth, his hands,
his throat, his bare back.

All of these thoughts sound like a pulsar. They're a rapid breathless beating percussion. What chance that any such life form will ever discover it, this golden disc, much less have any way of playing it, much less decode what the brainwaves mean? An infinitesimally small chance. Not a chance. But all the same the disc and its recordings will wander, trapped for eternity, around the Milky Way. In five billion years when the earth is long dead, it'll be a love song that outlives spent suns. The sound signature of a love-flooded brain, passing through the Oort Cloud, through solar systems, past hurtling meteorites, into the gravitational pull of stars that don't yet exist.

They watched yesterday the lunar rocket go cleanly into the night. They saw the fireball create a corona that lifted like a sudden sun, the ripping of the rocket boosters, a tower of smoke. Then the rocket forcing itself from the pandemonium of its launch and sailing up in effortless peace.

They'd followed the lunar astronauts each step of the way, they knew how it was for them, partly knew and partly imagined how they would feel. Disorientation for a few seconds on waking in their Cape Canaveral beach hut, followed by dawning, and then they'd sit up and swing their legs from the bed. From that moment onwards their thoughts would be clean and lean and they'd take a last shower and eat a last breakfast and go out of the beach hut to look at the sea and say not much.

The electric shark of a car had come to pick them up. When they got a first glimpse of their rocket high on its staging, its three boosters, twenty-seven engines, five million pounds of thrust, the look on their faces was the besotted sharp look of a street dog when it catches the scent of meat. Their families would refuse to wish them luck, knowing they were way beyond luck, in the launch-day zone of procedure and protocol, a weather briefing, one pill washed down for space sickness, another for pain relief, suit technicians waiting. Gloves on. 3D-printed helmet on. Retro superhero knee-high boots on. Leak-check the suit. Become flameproof and soundproof and vacuum-proof in a little cutting-edge bubble of simulated earth, should their capsule depressurise – but look a million dollars in a flatteringly tapered tux-like torso while the press take photos. You're James Bond, a Stormtrooper, you're Captain Marvel, you're Batgirl. Go to the launch pad, get in the reclining sculpted seat with its piped-in airflow that arrives at the thigh. Comms checks, hatch-leak checks, test all the relays and all of the loops and all of the hardware. Test them again.

At the beach hut they'd been human, a woman, a man, a wife and mother and daughter and a husband and father and son, and they'd crossed themselves, tapped their nails and bitten their lips in unconscious angst. But when they'd got to the launch pad they were Hollywood and sci-fi, *Space Odyssey* and Disney, imagineered, branded and ready. The rocket peaked in a cap of gleaming newness, absolute and spectacular whiteness and newness, and the sky was a glorious and conquerable blue.

Orbit 10

Some eighty million miles distant the sun is roaring. It edges now toward its eleven-or-so-year maximum, erupting and flashing, when you look you can see its edges are flayed with violent light and its surface sun-spot-bruised. Immense solar flares send proton storms earthwards and in their wake are geomagnetic storms triggering light displays three hundred miles high.

It's a radioactive soup out there and if their shields were to fail they'd be cooked and they know it. But a strange effect happens when the sun is so active, whereby its radiation (comparatively meek and resistible) pushes away cosmic radiation (a veritable bag of spitting snakes) and the soup that they swim in is thereby tempered. What their shields don't deflect the earth's magnetic fields do, and the dosimeter in the lab is barely per-turbed. The sun's particle clouds billow, flares explode and whip earthward in eight minutes flat, energy pulses, explodes, a great ball of fusion and fury. In the sun's fury they're somewhat and improbably cocooned, as if the sun were a dragon and they, by stupendous fortune, had found themselves in its domain and protection.

And in that leeside shelter here they are; it's early evening now: Shaun collecting the rubbish bags, Roman cleaning the Russian toilet and Pietro the US, Anton cleaning the air purification system, Chie wiping and disinfecting, Nell vacuuming the air vents, where she finds a pencil, a bolt and a screwdriver, some hair and some nail clippings.

Then a rare moment of aimlessness is upon them. Chie floats at the window portside knowing that their orbit is as far away from Japan as it can ever get; it'll be another four hours or so before they pass it again. My mother is there, she thinks. Everything that's left of my mother is there, and soon it will be burned and gone. They're skimming the very west of Africa, Mauritania, Mali now, soon Nigeria, Gabon, Angola; their second time of seeing these countries today, but this morning it was on the ascending orbit, this time they descend to skirt the coast and loop wide underneath the Cape of Good Hope like those ships of old.

Down over the arrowing peninsula of Dakar, crossing the equator, and in the closing minutes of day the lights of Brazzaville and Kinshasa on either side of the Congo

River tepid in the dusk. Blue becomes mauve becomes indigo becomes black, and night-time downs southern Africa in one. Gone is the paint-splattered, ink-leached, crumpled-satin, crumbled-pastel overflowing-fruit-bowl continent of chaotic perfection, the continent of salt pans and red sedimented floodplain and the nerve networks of splaying rivers and mountains that bubble up from the plains green and velvety like mould growth. Gone is a continent and here another sheer widow's veil of star-struck night.

Roman and Anton are in the Russian module, Roman trying to find a loose screw that floated out of a pair of scissors and is now somewhere about his head; Anton is at the window looking nadir, legs aloft. There are the disappearing lights of Cape Town and storms over the ocean. Wherever you are at night over the earth, there's always somewhere the soft erratic pulse of lightning. Electric silver-blue silent flower opening and closing. Here, over there, over here.

Absently Anton runs his fingers over a lump that's appeared on his neck the last fortnight and that he tries to obscure by raising the collar of his polo shirt. The last thing you need is to get sick in space. They'll worry and send you home and, because you can't fly back on your own, two others will have to go with you, and to cut short the missions of those two others would be unforgivable. He'll say nothing to the flight surgeon or to his fellow crew and he'll hope nobody notices. It's the size of a cherry in the low hollow of his neck, and perfectly painless.

There's his wife at home, herself so long unwell, and he's told their children he'll let nothing bad happen to any of them ever, as if such a thing were within his gift. He's the vehicle that carries them all through darkness, and the weight of that has borne him along for years and years. But he, too, is preyed on by darkness, as we all are. He never knew how to tell them that. He never knew how to say to his wife what he wanted amicably to say: *Zabudem, ladno?* Let's forget it, shall we? Let's call it a day. We don't love one another any more, why complicate what's simple? When he found the lump those were the words that came straight to his mind. *Zabudem, ladno?* They were casual and easy in his head as if he were proposing to end an awkward conversation. They were light words and they ended the decades of struggle inside him, and he feels sure that in the saying of the words they will all be released – he, his wife, their children – they will be released from the darkness he is supposed to and could never save them from.

The lovelessness of his marriage is a fact that has come upon him gradually, one gentle dawning after the other. When he's seen through a telescopic lens the flowlines made by ships pulling at the ocean, or the ancient shorelines of Bolivia's bright orange Laguna Colorada, or the red sulphur-stained tip of an erupting volcano, or the wind-cut folds of rock in the Kavir Desert, each sight has come to him as a winching open of the heart, a crack at a time. He'd not known how capacious it was, the heart. Nor how in love he could be with a ball of rock; it keeps him awake at night, the vitality of this love. Then, when he first caught sight of the lump on his neck it seemed – though he can't truly say why – the logical culmination of all those dawnings, those realisations that he and his wife didn't love each other and that life was too wide and too short. He's felt since then resolved, in possession of a crucial new piece of information. *Zabudem, ladno?* he'll say to his wife when he returns to earth, and she'll answer quickly without surprise and with a short nod, *Ladno, proekhali.* Let's. So easy an answer to a question they hadn't even known to ask. He tugs his collar stiffly up.

When Nell sees the lights of Cape Town she thinks of the time she went there as a child. She doesn't remember much of that trip, just, oddly, standing in a cobbled square in the heat with a tiny monkey on her shoulder, a monkey on a lead. Is that a real memory? She's sure the monkey-on-the-shoulder is real, and she knows she went to Cape Town, but she doesn't know if the two things belong together.

Pietro checks the news to see how far the typhoon has got; it unnerves him that they can no longer see it from their orbit. Meteorologists have decided upon calling it a super-typhoon; they speak of its rapid intensification that's left everyone ill-prepared, and of the increased regularity of storms like these. He goes to the observation dome to take photographs of the glistening sea and waxing moon, everything buffed and brushed and burnished. *God lays the beams of his upper chambers on the waters.* Psalm something-or-other, he remembers Shaun once telling him. And it does seem sometimes as though it could be true, this upper chamber that pours light on the seas. He takes photographs; hundreds.

What of the Filipino children he and his wife met on their honeymoon, the fisherman's children? Their easy toothy grins, the scuffed rough knees and silken skin, their vests and flip-flops and dirty toes, their sing-song chatter, the bottomless brown of their lovely eyes, their incomplete trust of these invading beings who had come to dinner and made them slack-jawed at photos of people in spacesuits, this ripped Buzz Lightyear in an Armani T-shirt, like they knew and saw what their parents didn't (or what their parents had chosen to overlook). That is, that the tables would never turn; that whatever universe Lightyear here and his tall nice-smelling and subtly pregnant wife had come from, they'd never see it, they'd never be sitting for dinner in the invaders' home on a luxury holiday with that one-day child, unless by some charitable favour they could never repay. And all the same and for all their distrust, the same measure of utter acceptance, of brimming giving, the gifts of shells they'd found, a green baseball cap (which Lightyear's wife wore for the rest of the evening), a plastic whistle in the shape of a donkey to give to their baby when it was born. Where are those children now; are they somewhere safe?

And then, when the day's experiments are done, they all six finish up the last of their tasks which is the rigorous documenting of their own selves; the appetite reports, the mood monitoring, the pulse measuring, the urine sampling. They each extract blood for the flight surgeon to analyse. This era is ebbing, Shaun thinks when he puts their vials of blood in the centrifuge for stowage. He thinks: the days of this trusty spaceship are numbered now. Why be confined to an orbit two hundred and fifty miles above the earth when you could be two hundred and fifty *thousand* miles above it? And

that's just the start. That's just the moon. Then a habitation base around the moon and a habitation base on
the moon, extended time spent there, with long-haul
spacecraft refuelling. One day not so distant there'll be
men and women slingshotting out of the earth's orbit
and away, away, far past the six of them here, toward the
beckoning red beacon of Mars.

This six, and those who've come before them, are
the lab rats who've made all things possible. They're the
specimens and the objects of research who've forged the
way for their own surpassing. One day their journeys to
space will seem nothing but a coach excursion, and the
horizons of possibility that open out at their fingers will
only confirm their own smallness and briefness. They
swim in microgravity like little watched fish. The heart
cells they culture will one day be used to replace those
of the slingshotting astronauts bound for Mars. But not
their own, which are fated to die. They take blood, urine,
faecal and saliva samples, monitor their heart rates and
blood pressure and sleep patterns, document any ache,
pain or unusual sensation. They are data. Above all else,
that. A means and not an end.

In its bareness, the thought brings them some relief
from the anguishes of space – the loneliness of being
here and the apprehension of leaving here. It was never

really about them and it is not about them now – what
they want, what they think, what they believe. Their
arrival and their return. It's about those four astronauts
on their way now to the moon, and the next men and
women, the men and women who will one day be going
to live on a new lunar station, those who will go into
deeper space, the decades of men and women who'll
come after them. Except it's not even about that, it's
just about the future and the siren song of other worlds,
some grand abstract dream of interplanetary life, of
humanity uncoupled from its hobbled earth and set
free; the conquest of the void.

The six here might or might not dream this dream
too, and it doesn't matter if they dream it, it doesn't matter, so long as they comply and play their parts. And
this they do gladly day in and out. They measure their
grip. They sleep with their chests constricted by straps
and monitors which hamper the breath. They scan their
brains. They swab their throats. They pull the syringe
from their overused veins. All of it gladly.

Maddening things:
  Forgetfulness
  Questions
  Church bells that ring every quarter-hour

Non-opening windows
Lying awake
Blocked noses
Hair in ducts and filters
Fire alarm tests
Powerlessness
A fly in the eye

In the Russian quarters there is an inflatable globe that wafts above the table; a picture on the wall of the Urals and another of the cosmonaut Alexei Leonov and another of Sergei Krikalev; the table cluttered with work tools hastily Velcroed, a fork in an empty can of tuna, Roman's amateur radio set-up. After more than twenty-five years and some one hundred and fifty thousand tearing orbits, the module is becoming old and creaky and less flight-worthy. On the outer shell of the craft, a crack has appeared. Slender, but troubling.

No gleaming capitalist Western space-dream here; no, a grey, utilitarian heftiness, a temple to sturdy engineering and the genius of the pragmatic. A time capsule of the post-Soviet years, the last echoes of a lapsed century. There is an attempt at home-making, to say this is a floor and this is a ceiling and this is the right way up, to defy the spaceness of space that dominates the other modules where up and down and left and right are vanished concepts. But its stab at cosiness is in vain, there's nothing cosy about Velcro walls and kilometres of cabling and flat buzzing light, and in the end it's neither space-age nor domestic – more a subterranean bunker which, all the same, they hold in great affection – for its efforts at comfort, failed though they are.

Here they gather this evening for dinner, the six of them, and Roman and Anton share out supplies from their larder – sorrel soup, borsch and *rassolnik*, potted fish, olives, cottage cheese and cubes of dried bread.

Was it just this morning that we talked about making the station look like a farmhouse? Pietro says. It feels either two minutes ago or otherwise five years, I can't decide. Maybe it's the typhoon, he says. The way it's tracked beneath us like some age-old beast.

Anton, near the observation window, looks out instinctively but there's no typhoon to see. He doesn't know where they are, it's all ocean and a blue and silver night. It's only when he spots a pinprick of light to starboard-side that he deduces Tasmania and gathers how far south they are now. The silhouette of the craft's robotic arm cuts diagonally across his view.

Nell brings a packet of chocolate-coated honeycomb that her husband sent up to her in the last resupply craft, because she was craving food that had a crunch and could not be scooped up with a spoon; he sent her three packs which she's been working through in morsels, the pleasure of eating it almost trumped by the pain of its being gone. She shares out the last of it among the crew; this paltry hoarding, no good, she thinks. They speak about things they miss – fresh doughnuts, fresh cream, roast potatoes. The sweets of their childhood.

I remember so well going to the *dagashiya* as a child, Chie says. We all went together after school, it was like another world – when you walked in there was a big counter full of candy, and candy was hanging from the ceiling and on all the walls, and the smell – the sweetness. It would make you faint if you stayed long enough. You would go in and ask for a mix. Some *bontan ame*, some *ninjin*, some candy cigarettes.

We would have a ten-pence mix-up, Nell says. If you chose carefully you could get sweets you could suck, and you could make them last all day.

Korovka, says Anton, thinking of his dream. And Roman echoes, Korovka.

Were those the sweets we had that time at your house? Pietro asks Roman. Your wife brought them out with coffee.

Roman affirms with a nod, Korovka.

Oh, those condensed-milk candies, Shaun says.

I loved those, Pietro says, they were the best part of the meal. No offence to your wife's cooking, Roman.

That *is* offensive to Roman's wife's cooking, Nell says.

Blackmail material, Chie says quietly.

Don't you think Russia is unduly afflicted with a love of condensed milk? says Shaun, who by now has floated above them as he likes to do, and hangs there picking honeycomb from his back teeth.

Your problem, in America, Roman says, is you don't put enough condensed milk in things. Actually that's the problem with the whole of the rest of the world.

Pietro tucks himself into a neat forward somersault on the way to the fridge. When I was a kid we had Galatine, perfect little milk candies, he says.

And Chie, wiping her mouth with a tissue she takes from her pocket, says, There are hardly any *dagashiya* left in Japan. They tend to have been turned into museums. It's all just convenience stores now.

Nell bats a piece of honeycomb from palm to palm and watches it glide as a shuttlecock might; Anton scrapes about with his fork at the last of the potted fish, so studious and serious, as to suggest that in that container is some depth or complexity the others can't see. Shaun, still above them, now floats on his back as if on the surface of water and looks at his hands, which are lately as soft as a child's, as soft as flannels.

The six of them barely register the gentle push backward as the spacecraft alters its course to avoid something, some space debris no doubt, the brief force of the thrusters lulling them slowly aft.

Chie says quite suddenly, My family have offered to wait and have the funeral when I arrive home, but I didn't want that, so it will be tomorrow.

She says she'll be there to scatter the ashes later in the Shikoko garden by the sea. And then she says, I can't stop thinking of home. Of my mother and father in their garden.

Shaun takes a napkin from the dispenser on the wall and hands it to her, though she isn't crying. She's distant when she takes it, as if she hasn't noticed him hand it over. The word *home* sits among them. The olive she'd had lined up in her chopsticks is dropped back into the sachet. Then she fastens her chopsticks to the table and begins to talk about a memory of her and her mother climbing a mountain in Shikoko. She gestures the immensity of the mountain with her arms, and then the napkin she still clutches becomes a waving flag. She says how her mother arrived at the top ahead of her, in the wind's full fury, and raised her arms in excitement and called *Chie-chan! Chie-chan! I'm here, I'm up here!* And that is the happiest memory she has of her mother as an adult, when her mother was strong and full of joy. It was the safest and most loved I had ever felt by her, Chie says. When she called out *Chie-chan! I'm up here!* I can't stop thinking of that now, she says.

When she falls quiet she tucks the napkin in her pocket. Maybe she's never spoken about herself this much in their handful of months together – nor in the years of training that went before. They're all some-what solitary and contained, but she more than any of them. Anton finds himself crying, and his tears form four droplets which float away from his eyes, and which he and Chie catch in the palms of their hands. They're not to let liquids loose in here and they're all fastidious about that.

Do you hear me? says Roman.

I hear you, the voice says.

That's good. I'm Roman.

Hello Roman, I'm Therese.

Therese, he says. I'm a Russian cosmonaut.

Wow. How's your English? My Russian isn't good.

Don't worry. Everybody's Russian isn't good.

I'm just outside Vancouver.

That's nice, I've been to Vancouver, a long time ago.

Well I've never been to space.

That's what I'd expect.

I wouldn't want to, you know.

We have just six or seven minutes before the orbit passes and the signal is lost, so maybe if you have a question?

Well, Roman, I guess I do.

I'm here.

Do you ever feel – do you ever feel crestfallen?

Crestfallen?

Yes. Do you ever?

I don't know the word, what does it mean?

What does it mean? It means, do you ever wonder what is the point?

Of being in space?

Of. Do you ever. Do you sometimes go to bed in space and think, why? Does it make you wonder? Or if you're cleaning your teeth when you're in space. I was once on a plane on a long-haul flight and I was cleaning my teeth in the washroom and I looked out the window and I suddenly thought, what's the point of my teeth? Not in a bad way, it just took the wind out of my sails to wonder what the point was of me, cleaning my teeth. It just stopped me there in my tracks. Can you understand me? Am I speaking too fast?

I understand.

And now sometimes, when I go to bed, I get the same feeling. That I'm pulling back the covers of my bed and I think of that time on the plane and the breath goes out of me. My shoulders go down, and I feel crestfallen. I feel sad. But I don't know why.

Crestfallen. It means – maybe depressed?

It means maybe disappointed. Dispirited. Yes, like the spirit goes out of you.

You want to know if that's how I feel?

Because I saw pictures of where you all sleep up there and it's just sleeping bags hanging in a little phone booth, and they looked so unwelcoming. So – absurd, if you don't mind me saying. And I wondered, did you get up there after all that effort – because I know it takes effort – and look at that and think, is this it? Didn't it seem an anticlimax? Do you know what I mean?

Absurd.

I've offended you.

No, no. I'm thinking.

I'm sorry.

I'll tell you something, Therese, about our sleeping bags. It's true that they hang, and most of us don't even fasten them with bungees to the wall, we hang freely and sail about, and it's very comforting. But my first night here I remember seeing my sleeping bag, and maybe at first sight you might be – what? – crestfallen, crestfallen to think this is your bed for several months, but then you see something and it makes you smile. I saw that it didn't quite hang, it isn't just hanging, you know – there's no gravity to make it, what's the word, heavy or—

Lifeless or limp.

That's it. You know, it *billows*; just slightly it billows like a ship's sail in a perfect wind. And you know, then, that so long as you stay in orbit you will be OK, you will not feel crestfallen, not once. You might miss home, you might be exhausted, you might feel like you're an animal in a cage, you might get lonely, but you will never, never be crestfallen.

It's like the spirit goes in you, then, not out of you. Like everything is alive? Like your sleeping bag is alive.

I think – yes, exactly.

I can't hear you well any more.

No.

I wish it were night so I could look up and see your light passing overhead.

We're passing nevertheless.

My husband died, this is his radio—

I'm sorry Therese, we're losing signal.

In the summer, he died.

I'm sorry, Therese—

Hello, are you there? Hello?

Love, I miss you, Shaun writes.

There's his wife's handwriting on the back of the *Las Meninas* postcard, her backward-slanting left-hand script tightly pressed, angular and masculine. This *missing*. And yet, if he were offered a trip home today no way would he take it, and when the time comes to go in several months, he won't wish to. An intoxication; the height-sick homesick drug of space. The simultaneous not wanting to be here and always wanting to be here, the heart scraped hollow with craving, which is not emptiness in the least, more the knowledge of how fillable he is. The sights from orbit do this; they make a billowing kite of you, given shape and loftiness by all that you aren't.

He lets the postcard float in the space above his laptop where it turns in slow balletic drift. At his email he has a question to answer for an editorial about the imminent moon landing; they've asked an actress, a physicist, a student, an artist, a writer, a biologist, a taxi driver, a nurse, a financier, an inventor, a film-maker, and an astronaut, himself, to respond: *with this new era of space travel, how are we writing the future of humanity?*

The future of humanity. Does he know anything about that? He thinks the taxi driver would have a better idea than he does. Over the years he feels he's whittled his mind down to a pinpoint through which he sees with absolute clarity the next few moments and is trained not to think of very much else.

When you spend a week deep in a cave system with four other people and very little food, crawling for hours through fissures that are barely larger than your own dimensions to see how much confinement you can withstand, and witness panic attacks in the sturdiest of people, you learn not to think beyond the next half-hour, let alone anything that could rightly be called *the future*. When you enter your spacesuit and try to habituate yourself to the difficulty moving, the painful chafing, the unscratchable itches that might persist for hours, to the disconnection, the sensation of being buried inside something you cannot get out of, of being inside a coffin, then you think only of your next breath, which must be shallow so as not to use too much oxygen, but not too shallow, and even the breath after that is of no concern, only this one. When you see the moon, or the pinkish tinge of Mars, you don't think about the future of humanity but only, if anything, the logistical likelihood of you or anyone you know being lucky enough to go there. You think of your own selfish obsessive brazen humanity, yourself elbow barging past thousands of others to get to the launch pad, because what else gave you an edge over those but the propulsion of a self-determination and belief that burns up everything else in its path?

With this new era of space travel, how are we writing the future of humanity?

The future of humanity is already written, he thinks.

There's perhaps never been so exciting and pivotal a time in space exploration, he begins to write.

When he sees Pietro move past, about to duck into his opposite quarters, he says, Pietro, with this new era of space travel, how are we writing the future of humanity?

Amidst the din of fans Pietro squints and cups his ears.

A little louder: With this new era of space travel, how are we writing the future of humanity?

The future of humanity? Pietro says.

Yep. How are we writing it?

With the gilded pens of billionaires, I guess.

Shaun smiles.

Did someone send you a postcard? Pietro jokes, coming to the doorway of Shaun's quarters and nodding at the *Las Meninas* that's in free-drift.

My wife, fifteen years ago, he says.

Pietro nods, and Shaun nips the postcard from its drift and hands it to him.

Read the back, Shaun says.

I wouldn't—

No, go ahead.

What is the subject of the painting? his wife has written on the postcard's reverse. *Who is looking at whom? The painter at the king and queen; the king and queen at themselves in a mirror; the viewer at the king and queen in the mirror; the viewer at the painter; the painter at the viewer, the viewer at the princess, the viewer at the ladies-in-waiting? Welcome to the labyrinth of mirrors that is human life.*

Is your wife always so obsessed with petty small-talk? Pietro asks.

And Shaun replies: I'm telling you, it's relentless.

Pietro stares for a while at the painting, and a while longer, then says, It's the dog.

Pardon?

To answer your wife's question, the subject of the painting is the dog.

He looks then – when Pietro hands back the postcard, reaches across to squeeze the bony dome of Shaun's shoulder before diving away – at the dog in the foreground. He'd never given it a second glance, but now he can't look at anything else. It has its eyes closed. In a painting that's all about looking and seeing, it's the only living thing in the scene that isn't looking anywhere, at anyone or anything. He sees now how large and handsome it is, and how prominent – and though it's dozing there's nothing slumped or dumb in that doze. Its paws are outstretched, its head erect and proud.

This can't be coincidental, he thinks, in so orchestrated and symbolic a scene, and it suddenly seems that Pietro is right, that he's understood the painting, or that his comment has made Shaun see a different painting altogether to the one he'd seen before. Now he doesn't see a painter or princess or dwarf or monarch, he sees a portrait of a dog. An animal surrounded by the strangeness of humans, all their odd cuffs and ruffles and silks and posturing, the mirrors and angles and viewpoints; all the ways they've tried not to be animals and how comical this is, when he looks at it now. And how the dog is the only thing in the painting that isn't slightly laughable or trapped within a matrix of vanities. The only thing in the painting that could be called vaguely free.

Orbit 11

Everything, everything is turning and passing.

So Shaun thinks and as he slips the postcard back in its pouch he feels like laughing at the question before him. *How are we writing the future of humanity?* We're not writing anything, it's writing us. We're windblown leaves. We think we're the wind, but we're just the leaf. And isn't it strange, how everything we do in our capacity as humans only asserts us more as the animals we are. Aren't we so insecure a species that we're forever gazing at ourselves and trying to ascertain what makes us different. We great ingenious curious beings who pioneer into space and change the future, when really the only thing humans can do that other animals cannot is start fire from nothing. That seems to be the only thing – and, granted, it's changed everything, but all the same. We're a few flint-strikes ahead of everything else, that's it. Chimps could do it if they watched us and learned, and before you know it they'd be gathering around fires and migrating to colder climes and cooking their food, and what do you know.

He offers a prayer, for the lunar astronauts, for Chie in her grief, for those in the path of the typhoon. A memory comes of a time in a nature reserve in Laos and of hearing the territorial morning duet of gibbons, a haunting looping song that carried through the canopies. When he thinks of the six of them here, or the astronauts now going to the moon, he hears that haunting call – that's what we're doing when we come into space, asserting our species by extending its territory. Space is the one remaining wilderness we have. The solar system into which we venture is just the new frontier now our earthly frontiers have been discovered and plundered. That's all this great human endeavour of space exploration really is, he thinks, an animal migration, a bid for survival. A looping song sent into the open, a territorial animal song.

With his eyes closed he can hear that gibbon call, hollow and echoing. Can see the dog in the painting in its private dignity. Imagines placing his hand on the warm neck of a horse and can feel the smooth, oily lie of its coat, though he's barely touched a horse in his life. The dart of a jay between the trees in his backyard. The dash of a spider into cover. The shadow of a pike beneath the water. A shrew carrying her young in her mouth. A hare leaping higher than seems warranted. A scarab beetle navigating by the stars.

Pick a single creature on this earth and its story will be the earth's story, he suddenly thinks. It can tell you everything, that one creature. The whole history of the world, the whole likely future of the world.

When Chie goes this evening to check on the mice, as she always does, she sees on the monitor that a miracle has happened – they're flying in circles. It's taken them a week but they've eschewed the grids in their cage and found their space-legs and have learned to negotiate microgravity. Now – is it joy or insanity? – they're rounding their shoebox module like little flying carpets. Joy, surely. It does look like joy. She goes to take them out of their modules unnecessarily, just for the sake of holding them.

It's then that she feels upon her the first complete closing in of grief. Not a stab or punch but something stealthy and suffocating, and she grasps the handrails and tries to breathe. The inside of the spacecraft is a whirring machine, she's living inside the workings of a clock and

it's grinding time through her bones, and her mother
is here on the top of that mountain with her blue and
white striped top and prim A-line skirt and walking boots
which give the sense that she's several ages at once, girl,
young mother, elderly woman, calling out with her sweet
deep voice.

Chie releases the handholds and folds herself into a
ball. She hangs this way. Her mother's funeral will be
moon-landing day, of all days. She lets the breath go out
of her. She might be making a strange sound but she
doesn't know because the noise of the module is over-
powering. Once you've mastered floating you can float
quite still without tipping. So she does. She drifts slowly
from one end of the module to the other with her knees
to her chin until she bumps gently against the hatch.
Then she ricochets back towards the module's centre.

Outside night drops a wing of dead black over the
mid-Atlantic and the planet vanishes.

There are times when it seems the only thing to do is
to tuck your legs to your chest and somersault through
the air. Shaun in the three cubic metres of space outside
his quarters. Nell and Pietro in the lab where they set up
a film to watch. Roman and Anton at a game of poker
in the Russian module, using as chips the disc magnets

which hold down their cards. Chie at the experiment rack where the mice are still flying. She opens her arms and windmills herself upside down.

Somersault, forward and back, with arms spread wide, recall the miracle of your weightlessness; remember that when you first came here you were baffled by the lack of gravity because your body kept wanting to decide which way was up, and nothing gave it any clue. It kept craving resistance and there was nothing to resist.

When they arrived here they had hours or days of space sickness. They kept crashing into things. They propelled themselves too fast or suddenly; the nausea drove them to hang in their quarters with a blindfold insisting to their brains they were lying down. But soon their bodies seemed to accept the change, and the acceptance was felt as a kind of peacekeeping. They dared a somersault. Then their minds followed and they began to understand – they hovered over the window with a day or night view of the earth and remembered with a fresh wave of comprehension that they were falling. They were weightless not through lack of gravity – there's plenty of gravity here, so close to earth – but because they were in a constant state of free fall. They were not flying, but falling. Falling at over seventeen thousand miles an hour. Never crashing of course; they could see what had only been theoretical before, that the earth was curving away from the hurtling free-falling craft at the exact rate the craft was travelling, so that the two could never collide. A game of cat and mouse. They inside, weightless in the sense that you're weightless for a moment on a plunging roller coaster. Working, running, sleeping, eating in a constant state of plummet.

They inside making somersaults backwards and forwards, because sometimes that's the only thing to do when you're falling and falling around the earth.

Orbit 12

They float in front of a Russian film about two cosmonauts whose bodies become possessed by aliens during
their re-entry to earth. They pass around a packet of
mints. By the end of the film the six of them are hanging,
arms raised straight in front of them, heads bobbing;
they look so peaceful in sleep.

Pietro with a faint smile, his hair thickly boyish, an
expression ever-hopeful. Nell's cheeks flushed and her
lips pursed as if she's still extracting the last taste of the
mint. Roman, heavy brows giving a sense of a deep purposeful contentment that must not be disturbed. Shaun,
looking somehow flung, his arms wider than the others',
his head tilted back. Chie, hands suspended from wrists
that seem breakable, an alertness in the movements of
her eyelids, ponytail wafting upright above her head as
always, but in sleep giving an odd pouncing sense of
readiness. Anton – Anton, looking pleased, as if he's just
presented his children with a much-wanted thing; his

hand is floating and the fist half-clenched, and a muscle twitches at the base of his thumb.

The film builds in sound at its climax, some thumping violence and searing music – but they are all well used to noise here. Nobody wakes.

Orbit 13

In the cosmic calendar of the universe and life, with the Big Bang happening on January 1st, almost fourteen billion years ago, when a supercharged universe-dense speck of energy blew open at the speed of faster-than-light and a thousand trillion degrees Celsius, an explosion that had to create the space it exploded into since there was no space, no something, no nothing, it was near the end of January that the first galaxies were born, almost a whole month and a billion years of atoms moving in cosmic commotion until they began to flock bombshell-bright in furnaces of hydrogen and helium we now call stars, the stars themselves flocking into galaxies until, almost two billion years later on March 16th, one of these galaxies, the Milky Way, was formed, and a six-billion-year summer passed in routine havoc until, at the end of August, a shockwave from a supernova might have caused a slowly rotating solar nebula to collapse – who knows? – but in any case it did collapse and in its condensed centre a star formed that we call our sun, and around it a disc of planets, in some cosmic clumping thumping clashing banging Wild West shootout of rock and gas and headlong combat of matter and gravity, and this is August.

Four days later the earth came about, and a day after that its moon.

September 14th, four billion years ago (or so some think) came life of sorts, some intrepid little single-celled things that invited themselves into existence in a moment of unthinking and didn't know the holy mess they'd make, and two weeks later on September 30th some of these bacteria learned to absorb infrared and produce sulphates and a month after that the greatest feat of all, to absorb visible light and produce oxygen, our breathable liveable lungable air, though the earth was still lungless for a long time yet, and on December 5th came multicellular life, red, brown and then finally green algae which spawned in boundless fluorescence in the shallows of sunlit water, and on December 20th plants found their way to the land, liverworts and mosses, stemless and rootless but there nonetheless, then hot on their heels only thousands of years later the vascular plants, grasses, ferns, cacti, trees, the earth's unbroken soil now root-snaked and tapped, plundered of moisture soon restocked by the clouds, looping systems of growth and rotting and growth again, competitive barging and elbowing for water and light, for height, for breadth, for greenness and colour.

Christmas Day, though Christ's not yet born – 0.23 billion years ago, and here come the dinosaurs for their five days of glory before the extinction event that wiped them out, or wiped out at least those landlubbing ones, the plodders and runners and tree-munchers, and left in their absence a vacant spot: *Wanted – land-dwelling life forms, no time-wasters, apply within*, and who should apply but the mammalian things, who quicksharp by mid-afternoon on New Year's Eve had evolved into their most opportunistic and crafty form, the igniters of fire, the hackers in stone, the melters of iron, the ploughers of earth, the worshippers of gods, the tellers of time, the sailors of ships, the wearers of shoes, the traders of grain, the discoverers of lands, the schemers of systems, the weavers of music, the singers of song, the mixers of paint, the binders of books, the crunchers of numbers, the slingers of arrows, the observers of atoms, the adorners of bodies, the gobblers of pills, the splitters of hairs, the scratchers of heads, the owners of minds, the losers of minds, the predators of everything, the arguers with death, the lovers of excess, the excess of love, the addled with love, the deficit of love, the lacking for love, the longing for love, the love of longing, the two-legged thing, the human being. Buddha came at six seconds to midnight, half a second later the Hindu gods, in another half-second came Christ and a second and a half later Allah.

In the closing second of the cosmic year there's industrialisation, fascism, the combustion engine, Augusto Pinochet, Nikola Tesla, Frida Kahlo, Malala Yousafzai, Alexander Hamilton, Viv Richards, Lucky Luciano, Ada Lovelace,

crowdfunding, the split atom, Pluto, surrealism, plastic, Einstein,

FloJo, Sitting Bull, Beatrix Potter, Indira Gandhi, Niels Bohr, Calamity Jane, Bob Dylan, Random Access Memory, soccer, pebble-dash, unfriending, the Russo-Japanese War, Coco Chanel,

antibiotics, the Burj Khalifa, Billie Holiday, Golda Meir, Igor Stravinsky, pizza,

Thermos flasks, the Cuban Missile Crisis,

thirty summer Olympics and twenty-four winter,

Katsushika Hokusai, Bashar Assad, Lady Gaga, Erik Satie, Muhammad Ali, the deep state, the world wars,

flying,

cyberspace, steel, transistors,

Kosovo, teabags, W. B. Yeats,

dark matter, jeans, the stock exchange, the Arab
Spring,
Virginia Woolf, Alberto Giacometti,
Usain Bolt, Johnny Cash,
birth control,
frozen food,
the sprung mattress,
the Higgs boson,
the moving image,
chess.

Except of course the universe doesn't end at the stroke
of midnight. Time moves on with its usual nihilism,
mows us all down, jaw-droppingly insensate to our pref-
erence for living. Guns us down. In another split second
millennia will pass and the beings on earth have become
exoskeletal-cybernetic-machine-deathless-postbeings
who've harnessed the energy of some hapless star and
are guzzling it dry.

If the cosmic calendar is in fact all of time, most of
which has not yet occurred, in another two months any
number of things could have happened to the cool marble of earth and none of them promising from a life point
of view – a wandering star could throw the whole solar
system out and earth with it, a meteor strike could cause
mass extinction, the earth's axial tilt could increase, the

flexing and drifting of orbits could eventually eject some planets, and in all events it'll be in roughly another four months, five billion years, that the sun will run out of fuel, expand to a red dwarf and consume Mercury and Venus. Earth, if it survives, will be scorched and arid, its oceans boiled dry, a cinder stuck in an interminable orbit of a white dwarf black dwarf dying sun until the whole show ends as the orbit decays and the sun eats us up.

And this is just the local scene; a minor scuffle, a mini-drama. We're caught in a universe of collision and drift, the long slow ripples of the first Big Bang as the cosmos breaks apart; the closest galaxies smash together, then those that are left scatter and flee one another until each is alone and there's only space, an expansion expanding into itself, an emptiness birthing itself, and in the cosmic calendar as it would exist then, all humans ever did and were will be a brief light that flickers on and off again one single day in the middle of the year, remembered by nothing.

We exist now in a fleeting bloom of life and knowing, one finger-snap of frantic being, and this is it. This summery burst of life is more bomb than bud. These fecund times are moving fast.

* * *

(Late, so late, the six crew awake discombobulated from their post-film sleep. Is it day or night? Have they got to the moon yet? What decade, what century are we in?

It's 1.30 a.m.; several hours past the rigidly scheduled bedtime. Lucky mission control turns the surveillance cameras off at night, they think, only half in jest; otherwise we'd all get it in the neck.

In this half-sleep and confusion the strangeness of their lives for a moment catches up with them. It finds them in a circle in the middle of the module facing each other as if they've just met again after a long time apart. Without word or reason they sail inwards and join, twelve arms interlinked. *Buona notte, o-yasumi, spakoynay nochee,* sweet dreams, goodnight. Hands squeezing shoulders and ruffling hair. Then propelling backwards, a brief look outside to bright daylight flooding Florida, and each of them off to their quarters, where the dark station thrums them back into sleep.)

Orbit 14, ascending

With untold peace and silence, the typhoon hits land. From the stillness of their vantage point, their solar arrays are copper against the night. The darkness of the Indian Ocean cedes to cloud which curdles, and the typhoon is a thick white mass sheened with moonlight. Their orbit proceeds north-east over Malaysia, Indonesia, the Philippines, but these islands are gone.

Nobody here is up to see it; it's past two in the morning and the spacecraft is dark and humming. Through the great domed window there's no view but a perspective-less expanse of typhoon. There's the easternmost arm of its spiral, and the clouds for hundreds of miles around have been whipped into motion. Anybody watching would be struck by vertigo at this swirling earth.

Those down there beneath the roof of cloud see a car door wing along a street followed by a sheet of corrugated iron. They see an uprooted tree smash into a bench itself smashed into a bike itself smashed up against a billboard that's blown across the road. They see fifty children huddled behind a barricade of desks while the school around them blows away. They see rain spearing into the floodwaters that surge inland. They see someone's dog washed down the street in two metres of soupy thing-thronged water, and the dog's someone following promptly after it, and a parasol, a pram, a book, a cupboard, dead birds, tarpaulin, a van, many shoes, coconut trees, a gate, a woman's body, a chair, roof timbers, Christ on his cross, a flag, countless bottles, a steering wheel, clothing, cats, door frames, bowls, road signs, you name it. They see the ocean roll over a town. The airport collapse, the planes capsize. The bridges give.

The very first crack of silver on the earth's right shoulder signals that dawn is soon to come, and as the orbit presses north the clouds are disbanding and the typhoon slopes away behind. The lights of Taiwan and Hong Kong rounding towards them on the earth's curvature look like fires raging. The ring of airglow at the atmosphere is neon green fading to orange.

Now some dreams come to Chie in which her mother is alive; they're spiked with relief and exultation. Beneath her Japan and East Asia crowd the forward view and if she were to wake and look out she'd see little or nothing of the typhoon. She'd see only a lovely planet shifting unfalteringly past the places of her childhood. It's the last of night down there and the continent is etched in gold.

Orbit 14, descending

Anticipated things:
  Plums
  O-nigiri
  Skiing
  Slamming a door in anger
  Sore feet
  Fried eggs
  Frog calls
  Need of a thick winter coat
  Weather

Making lists is what Chie would do when she was a child, when she was disturbed or anxious. She went through a phase of unexplained anger, and began to write lists of all the people she would like to be rid of, and all the ways she'd like them to die. She knew it was wrong to want to kill them herself, so their deaths were always preventable accidents. When the anger subsided the lists changed in mood but didn't cease to be. Her parents supposed it was her way of controlling her feelings and never tried to stop her, and barely made comment, and all her life, in difficult times, the lists resurface. In some ways she hardly notices herself writing them, they're like nail-biting or teeth-grinding, they bring a reflexive comfort. Here, they waft slightly on their pegs in her sleeping quarters while she dreams. Once, when she was around eight years old, she wrote a list of *unusual things*, one item of which was female pilots. She asked her parents, her teachers, how many female pilots there were in Japan and the answer turned out to be none, in the military at least. None. And a seed was sown in a resolute mind, a methodical and fearless and crystalline mind.

When Anton was a child of six or seven, he made a model of a spaceship as many children are wont to do, out of a washing-up-liquid bottle and tinfoil, and his astronauts, who were fashioned from pegs and swaddled in cotton wool, made spacewalks almost daily. They were permanently dressed for a spacewalk, white and so puffy as to be near limbless, and they popped from the hatch within seconds of waking, as easily as slipping out of bed. His father showed him that if he sat in a dark room and shone a torchlight, it was often possible to see the glittery suspension of dust motes in the path of the light; it was into these that his astronauts would launch, and he would hold them lightly between thumb and forefinger and let them float among the dust motes as if among stars. And this soon became the purpose of the spacewalks – to catalogue an ever deeper field of stars.

In her dreams now, Nell is swimming with Shaun in search of the *Challenger* astronauts, except that Nell is a child, at least that's what the dream tells her; she doesn't look like a child, she looks like herself, but since herself is somewhat elfin it's easy for the dream to transpose the two, child and adult; they're diving. Nell has a candle whose flame flutters in the water. Then they find it, the thing they were looking for, which turns out to be a fire. On the seabed, a bonfire. Its flame is circular as are flames in microgravity, and they take it with them back to a boat which in fact is a rock bobbing in the middle of the ocean. On this rock is her mother holding the small monkey that Nell remembered today, the monkey in the memory of the square in Cape Town, and which in the dream seems fresh and full of meaning. Ah, Nell thinks, I see. I see at last; this is why I came to space. There's a shock of grief that detonates her dream and blows it to pieces. She wakes. She doesn't know what it is she understood in the dream, it's there in her mind but vanishes on contact. There's just an age-old grief for her long-dead mother. No longer unhappy, just an abrasion.

When she drifts back towards sleep the mother she sees is not her own but Chie's.

The peculiar thing (that they'll never discover) is that Shaun is dreaming too of this circular flame, this microgravity doughnut of fire. Not the rest, just the fire. It's spinning in space and it perturbs him because it seems to disprove the existence of God, in some logic that belongs only to dreams. Then the doughnut of fire becomes a typhoon, a little spiral thing that looks just like a galaxy, and he's watching it distantly. At some point in the night he's taken his earplugs out and is holding them one in each gently closed hand.

I decided to be an astronaut when I was in the womb, Roman's saying to a roomful of people. Before I was born, when I was taking in oxygen through an umbilical cord, when I was swimming weightless, when I knew infinity because I'd recently come from it, that's when I decided to become an astronaut. And the people in the room start laughing and clapping as if he's told a joke, when in fact he's told the plainest truth he knows. All the same, he feels exceptionally happy. His mother and father are in the room, clapping along, and behind them Anton.

Chie, half awake and half asleep, is down in Shikoku in her parents' house by the sea and a typhoon is howling and the moon is blown sideways. She's on the porch steps holding her mother tight to her chest and her mother is a child and her hands in Chie's are small as mikans. The sea is lapping at the bottom step. *It's alright, mother*, she whispers, *daijōbu-desu, there, it's alright. It's moon-landing day, she says, look up and see.* But what they see is that the moon, towards which the astronauts are sailing, has been blown half an earth-orbit off course and the astronauts can't find it, to which her mother says, *I always knew that would happen. I always knew it.* She holds her mother while the millennia pass, crushing her into her chest. I shouldn't have left you, she's thinking. I shall never again go away so far. The planets whip about the earth and the light is orange and the earth collides with the windblown moon, and they stay on their step. *I shall never again*, she says, *I shall never again.*

For Anton there's the moon dream once again, its third repeat. He's drifting alone near the moon as Michael Collins had, and he hears a murmur, and this time it doesn't turn into voices but into music, a violin's note which stretches space so that the earth is so far away he can barely see it. Everything warps with music. He is in love; he doesn't question with whom or what, or how he knows, but he knows, and he climbs out of his spacesuit the better to feel it, this elastic ecstatic thing;

he removes the helmet of his spacesuit to find it was only ever a hat, a silk *kartuz* hat topped with a large red flower.

Pietro doesn't dream. He has a rare night of deep and solid unthinking sleep. His breaths and heartbeats are smooth and few, his face resolved of its creases, his body a well of atom-self, an unworried sum of parts, as if he knows that outside the earth falls away in perpetual invention and leaves nothing more for him to do. Our lives here are inexpressibly trivial and momentous at once, it seems he's about to wake up and say. Both repetitive and unprecedented. We matter greatly and not at all. To reach some pinnacle of human achievement only to discover that your achievements are next to nothing and that to understand this is the greatest achievement of any life, which itself is nothing, and also much more than everything. Some metal separates us from the void; death is so close. Life is everywhere, everywhere.

Orbit 15

They've been sailing north-east in darkness from the Antarctic ice shelf, across acres of unwitnessed nothing. Everyone sleeps. Beneath glides the Indian Ocean at night, with barely a sense of the earth's existence. There's the faded orange line of the atmosphere which is the only suggestion that a planet is there – that and the close and faithful moon. Yet through the atmosphere the stars can be seen, and so it seems that this outer edge of the earth is made of glass, or that the planet is contained inside a glass dome. And as their spacecraft orbits toward an ever-renewing horizon, so the stars seem to rush and fizz in their billions upwards.

Perhaps this spacecraft is the only thing. Silently sliding around an invisible rock. Perhaps it was this way for those early discoverers who, on a blind night at sea, many months and thousands of miles from a coast they couldn't yet be sure existed, had been filled with an intimacy with the earth, some sense that they were the only ones on it, and had known a brief peace.

It's just gone three in the morning on the clocks up here. Down there lightning pulses slow and dazzling from the black, tens or hundreds of miles apart, and the satin dark turns milky with storm cloud. The equator nears. It brings a shrieking star, a huge Bethlehem light. It's not so much that they follow it as that it comes for them, a wave of dawn that washes night to the aft, and the clouds (the debris of a wrecked typhoon) are turbulent peaks of violet and peach.

The hundred-cymbal clang of sudden daylight. A few minutes later they come in off the ocean where the Maldives, Sri Lanka, the tip of India are ripe with morning. The shallow shoals and sandbanks of the Gulf of Mannar. Off to starboard are the shores of Malaysia and Indonesia where the sand, algae, coral and phytoplankton make the water luminous with a spectrum of greens – except now there's tumbled broken-up storm cloud and the usually tranquil view is weary and troubled. As they ascend India's east coast the clouds are thinning; morning strengthens, is briefly stark, and then a haze moves in at the Bay of Bengal, the clouds wispy and numerous and the Ganges silt estuary opens into Bangladesh. The umber plains and ochre rivers, burgundy valley of a thousand-mile ridge. The Himalayas are a creeping hoar frost; Everest an indiscernible blip.

Everything beyond them, which caps the earth, is the rich fresh brown of the Tibetan Plateau, glacial, river-run and studded with sapphire frozen lakes.

Up now and diagonally across China's great mountains, the faint smudge of rust that is the extraordinary autumn bloom of the Jiuzhaigou Valley and then the Gobi Desert in seeming plainness, except in looking closer there are the fearless brushstrokes of a painter who sees in sand the movement of water and sees in brown bolts of duck-egg mauve lemon and crimson, and casts the arid in shades of oil spill, and makes of canyons nacreous shells. And on it presses, the northward orbit, into the afternoon of North Korea and up above Hokkaido. Japan is a wisp trailing into a vanishing point. It was eleven orbits and sixteen hours ago that they passed it going down, and this time they skim it going up, across the arm of Russian islands that sweep along the Pacific ridge, over the Bering Sea. Now the land falls away like a silken slip.

There is the feeling of climbing over the continents, climbing up and over the crest of the earth. Up and over the north Pacific in a wide clean arc. Though their orbit proceeds in a straight line around the planet, the planet's turn makes the orbital path appear to loop up and down, north and south in deep undulations, from the rim of the Arctic Circle to the southern seas. And now, at its northernmost point, it dips again. Far off to the left is the smooth, crisp bonbon of ice that marks Alaska. A cloud-free confection of crackable white. When the cloud accrues further south, the whole of the view is a liquid swirl of ice floe and cloud. The long tail of the Alaska Peninsula. A glimpse of land, of fjord and inlet. Spine of mountain range. Ice floe thinning. The coast of Canada portside not a coast at all but a land that's been sledgehammered into random pieces.

Before they came here there used to be a sense of the other side of the world, a far-away-and-out-of-reach. Now they see how the continents run into each other like overgrown gardens – that Asia and Australasia are not separate at all but are made continuous by the islands that trail between; likewise Russia and Alaska are nose to nose, barely a spit of water to hold them apart. Europe runs into Asia with not a note of fanfare. Continents and countries come one after the other and the earth feels – not small, but almost endlessly connected, an epic poem of flowing verses. It holds no possibility of opposition. And even when the oceans come, and come and come and come in a seamless reel, and there's no sense of land or anything but polished blue, and every country you've ever heard of seems to have slid into the cavern of space, even then there's no waiting for anything else. There is nothing else and never was. When land comes again you think, oh yes, as if you've just woken up from a captivating dream. And when ocean comes again you think, oh yes, as if you've woken up from a dream in a dream, until you're so dream-packed that you can find no way out and don't think to try. You're just floating and spinning and flying a hundred miles deep inside a dream.

The night is over there. Off to the east, where the horizon is blurring. Not here yet but they're tracking closer. The Pacific below, and falling away in a warped curve are the snow-dusted peaks of the Sierra Nevada, and if you looked through a zoom lens you'd see, far off, San Francisco, Los Angeles, San Diego imprinted on a landmass that's imprinted on sea, a coastline drawn in sharp-tipped white, a greyish hue of singed shrubland. The fertile coastal plains of the Baja California. Central America's scrawny neck. Then they too warp away.

There are times when the rapidity of this passage across the earth is enough to exhaust and bewilder. You leave one continent and are at the next within quarter of an hour, and it's hard sometimes to shake the sense of that vanished continent, it sits on your back, all the life that happens there which came and went. The continents pass by like fields and villages from the window of a train. Days and nights, seasons and stars, democracies and dictatorships. It's only at night when you sleep that you're relieved of this perpetual treadmill. And even when you sleep you feel the earth turning, just as you feel a person lying next to you. You feel it there. You feel all the days that break through your seven-hour night. You feel all the fizzing stars and the moods of the oceans and the lurch of the light through your skin, and if the earth were to pause for a second on its orbit, you'd wake with a start knowing something was wrong.

Forty minutes have passed since dawn and sidling in now from the east is the shadow of night. It seems not much, just a portside smudge. Blue has turned purple but that's about it. Green has turned purple, white has turned purple, America has turned purple, or what's left of it anyway. No, America has gone. Night has un-ravelled the earth's blue-green weave. The equator is crossed again from north to south and the moon is dusky and one degree fatter. Suddenly now, as if displeased, the Terminator swipes daylight off the face of the earth and the stars burst up like snowdrops from God knows where. In their sleep the crew feel the abrupt weight of night – someone has turned off that great bulb of a planet. They fall a notch deeper into sleep.

Ocean now, the South Pacific off the shores of Ecuador and Peru where Quito and Lima herald the land. There are a thousand miles of lightning zapping the coast, and a two-thousand-mile trail of nimbus cloud that sits on the sea, and a four-thousand-mile rampart of mountain. And in the densest dark where there are no cities, there's a thousand-mile patchwork of orange dots where the rainforest burns. It burns right up to the edge of the Andes. It burns right across to eastern Brazil and down to Paraguay and Argentina, where the orbit crosses a continent on fire. Twelve million lives are nestled below in Buenos Aires, where centre gives to suburb gives to farmland gives to black, and where river gives to estuary gives to ocean, and the high Antarctic Circle.

Tucked under the belly of the earth, in all these hectares of night, is the odd ambience of the South Pole in twilight, but here at these more northerly latitudes the sky is thick and full of galaxy. You are looking now straight into the heart of the Milky Way, whose pull is so strong and compelling that it feels some nights that the orbit will detach from the earth and venture there, into that deep, dense mass of stars. Billions upon billions of stars that give off their own light, so that it's no longer true to speak of darkness.

Now there's the long pass of the South Atlantic un-interrupted by land for some two thousand miles until the southernmost tip of Africa. But if the crew were watching and had adjusted their eyes, there'd be no sense of emptiness, only the immense consolation of that which they could never fathom or comprehend. And it's through this night that their craft sails for a time, lost in the world.

When the lights of Cape Town come they're a talon that marks the beginning, or end, of a continent of several thousand miles. The ascending orbit moves up its coast, Mozambique, Tanzania, Kenya, Somalia. Africa is dusty brown in the moonlit night, sparsely clouded, and electrified by lightning across its breadth. Its city lights are discreet and scant. Maputo here, Harare there, Lusaka over there, Mombasa ahead, and each is a small heap of gold coins on a tapestried cloth, joined by nothing – no night-lit roads or urban sprawl. A beautiful velvety poverty of man on an earth that tips into the void; you feel you'd fall off, except with each new moment there's yet more earth, and you follow its trail across the Gulf of Aden to the Middle East.

The lights of Salalah on the Arabian Sea, electric screech in soft swirling desert, and a minute earlier Abu Dhabi, Doha, Muscat would have bejewelled the far coast but time is up – the sun is coming one more time and a shank of silver skewers open the night. For the crew there've been thousands of sunrises while they've been in space, and of those they've watched hundreds, and if they were awake now they'd float from their quarters and watch another. They don't know how it can be that their view is so endlessly repetitive and yet each time, every single time, newly born. They'd open the shutters of the domed windows, and become aware of themselves as a solitary head and torso in the vacuum of space. Suspended in a little pocket of breathable air. A sense of gratitude so overwhelming that there'd be nothing they could do with or about it, no word or thought that could be its equal, so for a moment they'd close their eyes. The earth would still be there on the inside of the eyelids, a vivid and geometrically perfect sphere, and they'd have no idea if this was simply an after-image or a projection of the mind, which knew that planet so well by now that it could draw it without reference.

With each sunrise nothing is diminished or lost and every single one staggers them. Every single time that blade of light cracks open and the sun explodes from it, a momentary immaculate star, then spills its light like a pail upended, and floods the earth, every time night becomes day in a matter of a minute, every time the earth dips through space like a creature diving and finds another day, day after day after day from the depth of space, a day every ninety minutes, every day brand new and of infinite supply, it staggers them.

And now those cities on the Gulf of Oman are passing behind, blanched by dawn. Rose-flushed mountains, lavender desert, and up ahead Afghanistan, Uzbekistan, Kazakhstan, and a round of faint cloud that is the moon. Sometimes when they pass over Kazakhstan they can't properly assimilate the fact that they left earth from there, and will go back to there. That the only means of getting home is to rip through the atmosphere in flames, glass blackened, to pray that the heat shield holds and that the parachutes and reverse thrusters deploy, and that all of the thousands of moving, working parts move and work. It's difficult to compute that the whispering line man calls the atmosphere is a thing they must crash through. That they must burn and roll in a blazing ball before they jolt up with the drogue and see the grasses and wild horses of the Kazakh plains.

In their sleep the crew has gone one more full ninety-minute transit around the earth, their fifteenth orbit of the day's sixteen. To starboard now the view is only the snow-covered Himalayas that stretch away like a road, a vast, open and endless road. To the south of those mountains are cities, Lahore and New Delhi, which in the brilliance of day will have bleached into the land-scape, gone. Eaten up by a topography of wilderness that doesn't seem to know mankind. Just that mountain range leading ever south.

It's mid-morning coming in to Russia and in the shrill light the earth is once again a glass marble in blackest space. Bereft and fragile now that its neighbouring stars and planets can no longer be seen. And yet it is, at the same time, the opposite of fragile. There's nothing there on its flawless surface that could break, and it's as if there is in fact nothing there at all – the more you look at it the less substance it has and the more it becomes an apparition, a holy ghost.

The whole globe has passed beneath and will keep on passing. With each full orbit they'll track a few degrees westward, and when the orbit comes north again in another ninety minutes it will be over Eastern Europe, where yet another day will break. Another fresh day in all the fresh days. The earth is blue-hooped and covered with snow. The orbit is almost as far north as it will ever be and begins to round out at the lower edge of the Arctic Circle. Beyond, the North Pole which is never quite seen. Descending now away from Russia and toward a Pacific passage of five thousand miles.

Orbit 16

By now the lunar astronauts are journeying in their little thimble of a command module towards moon orbit. They're entering the first stage of their powered flyby. Did you know, says Capcom from ground control, that the record for the most lightning strikes sustained by one person has been broken? It was seven strikes, but as of last week a man in China has been struck by lightning eight times. Oh, says one of the lunar crew, does he carry a lightning rod around with him? The things people will do to break a record, laughs another, and Capcom tells them that eighty-four per cent of deaths by lightning strike are men. That figures, says one of the female crew. Live dumb, die young. What happened, by the way, to that thing you told us last night, about the cow that got stuck in a peat bog? They hoisted it out, Capcom says. It was there all day but they got some straps and a Mitsubishi pickup and pulled the thing out. Hope it obliged them with a little milk at the end of that. How's the moon looking from where you are? It looks shadowed and grey like a fat old man, they say. It looks bashed up but all the same kind of welcoming. We can just about see where we'll land when we reach the South Pole. It's more stunning than we'd ever hoped. We'll have you there safe and sound in the next nine hours, Capcom tells them. God willing and with a good wind behind us, one says, and another adds: All that effort to save a cow.

From an outside view you'd see them wend a long-untrodden man-made trail between two birling spheres. You'd see that far from venturing out alone, they navigate through a swarm of satellites, a midgey seething of orbiting things, two hundred million flung-out things. Operating satellites, ex-satellites blown into pieces, natural satellites, flecks of paint, frozen engine coolant, the upper stages of rockets, bits of *Sputnik 1* and *Iridium 33* and *Kosmos 2251*, solid-rocket exhaust particles, a lost toolbag, a mislaid camera, a dropped pair of pliers and a pair of gloves. Two hundred million things orbiting at twenty-five thousand miles an hour and sandblasting the veneer of space.

From an outside view you'd see the lunar spaceship tiptoe its way through this field of junk. It negotiates through low earth orbit, the busiest and trashiest stretch of the solar system, and with an injection burn it forces itself out on its transit to the moon where the clutter thins and the going's fair. A full-throttle scarper in their billionaire's rocket, out and away, away from the junk, away from the breaking burning storming scintillating earth like fleeing the scene of a crime. Away from the plucking flinging brute typhoon and the houses barging down roads become rapids and calamitous ruin that can't yet be measured. Away from the planet held hostage by humans, a gun to its vitals, teetering slightly on its canting orbit, away into virgin up-for-sale wilderness, this new black gold, this new domain ripe for the taking. Through their quarter-of-a-million-mile sward of space.

Here sleep Anton, Roman, Nell, Chie, Shaun and Pietro in tubular modules that are daily pelted and barraged and pitted with dents. They hang like bats in their quarters. Anton wakes briefly with his fist in his cheek. His first and only thought is of the spacecraft on its way to the moon, accompanied by one piercing feeling of childhood joy which pops like a bubble as he drops back to sleep. On Pietro's monitor that's fastened to the rigging near his head, a message has come up in silence from his wife with a link to a news story about the terrible destruction of the typhoon, which will stay there unread until morning. An unread message on Shaun's screen too, a video of a goat jumping on a trampoline, from his daughter, with no caption except *ILY!*

The modules are dark and shuttered. The robotic workstation, the resistance trainer, the computers with their timelines of work for the following day that are being uploaded now from the ground; the cameras and microscopes, the piles of cargo bags, the experiment gloveboxes, the bio-product lab and its module of mice, the *pond* where their bags of water are stowed, Anton's cabbages and pea shoots, the suits in the airlock, nodding crudely human puppets giving off the burnt smell of space.

It's almost five in the morning and Roman knows in this light band of pre-alarm sleep that they'll be circling now somewhere near Turkmenistan, Uzbekistan, which means that south-western Russia will be distant portside, that outlying hook between the Black and Caspian Seas. Overnight the cities have been laid down in the season's first fine snow – Samara and Tolyatti on the gorged banks of the Volga, a black snake hulking through white.

It's as if each orbit is encoded into him. He's been up here almost half a year now and he knows the paths they take over the earth, the procession of orbits, their repeating patterns. Even in sleep he's remotely aware of the sun glinting off the gold domes of Tolyatti's cathedral – a flash of light that seems to appear from nothing. A little way south the triangular shape of Volgograd, which they see from above when they fly from Star City to Kazakhstan for their launch; when you see Volgograd from the plane you know you're near the Kazakhstan border and leaving Russia and everything and everyone behind.

The crack that's appeared outside gives a millimetre or two. It sends out fissures that broadly echo an aerial map of the confluencing Volga River. It's not so far from Roman's head, this crack, on the other side of the thin alloy shell, and no patching with epoxy and Kapton tape is going to hold it. The pressure in the Russian module drops just a fraction, barely noticeable, not enough to sound any alarm, and the clocks count themselves round towards waking time and the onset of another blitzed and man-made day.

When you've moved along the length of the space-ship to its aft, through hatches that get ever smaller and modules that get ever older, and you've come here to the decrepit Soviet bunker right at the end where Anton and Roman sleep, then you see the table still littered from dinner (a bad habit of this crew to leave their clearing up to the next day) – there are some spoons fastened with Velcro, and fastened next to them two empty vacuum-packed sachets of olives, the sachets now stuffed with napkins that are splattered with borsch, there are four idly spinning crumbs of honeycomb that have been caught for now in an equilibrium of forces between the module's air vents which push them one way and the spacecraft's air vents that pull them the other, and below where they float there are some unopened packets of bread cubes pegged to the wall.

A foot or so beyond those four suspended crumbs is the photograph of Roman's hero, Sergei Krikalev – thin, neat and inscrutable, small-eared, blue-eyed, slight melancholia about the face, a touch of the Mona Lisa smile. It was he, Krikalev, who was one of the first two humans up here in this craft and it was he who first turned on the lights which ebbed through windows into the bare dark.

He seems to know that something is ending, that all good things must go this way, towards fracture and fallout. So many astronauts and cosmonauts have passed through here, this orbiting laboratory, this science experiment in the carefully controlled nurturing of peace. It's going to end. And it will end through the restless spirit of endeavour that made it possible in the first place. Striking out, further and deeper. The moon, the moon. Mars, the moon. Further yet. A human being was not made to stand still.

Maybe we're the new dinosaurs and need to watch out. But then maybe against all the odds we'll migrate to Mars where we'll start a colony of gentle preservers, people who'll want to keep the red planet red, we'll devise a planetary flag because that's a thing we lacked on earth and we've come to wonder if that's why it all fell apart, and we'll look back at the faint dot of blue that is our old convalescing earth and we'll say, Do you remember? Have you heard the tales? Maybe there's another parent-planet – earth was our mother and Mars, or somewhere, will be our father. We are not such orphans-in-waiting after all.

Krikalev seems to look out now from the photograph as a god looks on its creation, with a patient forbearance. Humankind is a band of sailors, he's thinking, a brotherhood of sailors out on the oceans. Humankind is not this nation or that, it is all together, always together come what may. He sits in timeless stillness amid the module's perpetual eighty-decibel machine vibration while around him the green Velcroed flammable walls close in airlessly. And each day and week the crack on its hull widens and Krikalev's smile seems more and more vaunted and more and more godly.

Let there be light, he seems quietly to say.

Forty or fifty bodies are sheltered behind the altar of a chapel which squats low among trees. Floodwater

reaches to its roof. The mile of coconut plantation between here and the coast is submerged completely by
the tidal surge, but the buffering of the trees has saved
the chapel; by design it has no windows along its east
elevation which is toward the ocean and those elsewhere
are so far spared. The chapel door strains but holds under
the burden of water. The concrete walls crack, but they
hold too. Hunks of plaster fall from the ceiling under the
stooping timbers. A dead shark tumbles past the front
window. The wind is ebbing. The people inside no longer hear it slamming against the roof. If the building
can withstand the flood for another few hours until the
water recedes they'll make it. They pray.

It's the Santo Niño that's saving them, they're inclined
to believe. Even the non- or less religious think it now.
Gathered around this little embroidered effigy of the
child Jesus, praying and praying, praying for hours,
turning away from the ocean that leans on the windows, whispering and muttering and clutching each
other, they suppose they must be witnessing a miracle.
They don't know how else the building could stand. It
isn't possible. Far bigger and more robust buildings will
have collapsed in the rampage of this typhoon. But if
the Santo Niño remains in its glass casing intact then
they'll remain intact too. They've taken it from its ledge

and huddled around and they daren't move; somehow a few of their children who'd been wailing in fear are now sound asleep.

The fisherman's wife has one child in her cross-legged lap and another propped against her. The other two children are curled asleep with their heads in the fisherman's lap, his right hand laid quietly on one forehead, left on the other. His wife has a gash across her shoulder from a sheet of metal as they were fleeing, which she bears without complaint. An unearthly watery light fills the chapel, a smell of brine and wet wood. The children are safe. The sea has stopped surging, it rests exhausted. The wind is ebbing.

From space the Philippines and Indonesia are shrouded now in fine arrangements of cloud in multiple vortices and eddies that soon will push westward. The typhoon has smashed itself to pieces against the land. The islands are smaller than they were several hours ago, misshapen by flood. The worst is gone.

From the east shunts a bright front of unforgiving heat rolling in off the Pacific, which, from the last descent of this sixteenth orbit, is a glorious coppering of disbanded light. It isn't water, it isn't earth, it's only photons and it can't be grasped and it can't remain. It starts to unpick as night falls steep across the tranche of the Southern Pacific.

One day a few years hence, at this very spot in the Pacific that it's passing now, this craft will bow graciously out of orbit and plummet through the atmosphere into the ocean. Submarines will go down to explore its wreckage. But that's another thirty-five thousand orbits away. This orbit reaches its deepest edge where auroras flicker across Antarctica and the moon rises huge as a buckled bicycle wheel. It's 5.30 a.m. Wednesday morning; moon-landing day. The stars explode.

Out there, electromagnetic vibrations ripple through the vacuum as bodies in space give out light. If these vibrations are translated into sounds then the planets each have their own music, the sound of their light. The sound of their magnetic fields and ionospheres, their solar winds, the radio waves trapped between the planet and its atmosphere.

Neptune's sound is liquid and rushing, a tide crashing onto a shore in a howling storm; Saturn's is that of the sonic boom of a jet, a sound that resonates up through your feet and between the bones; Saturn's rings are different still, a gale siphoning through a derelict building but in slowed and warping tempo. Uranus a frantic zapping screech. Jupiter's moon, Io, makes the metallic pulsing hum of a tuning fork.

And the earth, a complex orchestra of sounds, an out-of-tune band practice of saws and woodwind, a spacey full-throttle distortion of engines, a speed-of-light battle between galactic tribes, a ricochet of trills from a damp rainforest morning, the opening bars of electronic trance, and behind it all a ringing sound, a sound gathered in a hollow throat. A fumbled harmony taking shape. The sound of very far-off voices coming together in a choral mass, an angelic sustained note that expands through the static. You think it'll burst into song, the way the choral sound emerges full of intent, and this polished-bead planet sounds briefly so sweet. Its light is a choir. Its light is an ensemble of a trillion things which rally and unify for a few short moments before falling back into the rin-tin-tin and jumbled tumbling of static galactic woodwind rainforest trance of a wild and lilting world.

Acknowledgements

With gratitude to NASA and ESA for the wealth of information made available. And for the various gifts of support: the Society of Authors, the Santa Maddalena Foundation, Yaro Savelyeva, Paul Lynch, Max Porter, Nathan Filer, Al Halcrow, Seren Adams, Dana Friis, Rick Hewes, Anna Webber, Elisabeth Schmitz, Lilly Sandberg, Zeljka Marosevic, David Milner, Emma Lopes, Michal Shavit, and Dan Franklin (for getting me this far) – thank you, so much.